Just Something in the Wind

—An Abemly Shores Novel—

Gail Wallach Buell

—Beaver's Pond Press—
Minneapolis, MN

Edited by Angela Wiechmann

ISBN 13: 978-1-64343-994-5
Library of Congress Catalog Number: 2018963898
Printed in the United States of America
First Printing: 2019
23 22 21 20 19   5 4 3 2 1

Cover artwork created by Nate Peterson,
www.npdesignphotography.com

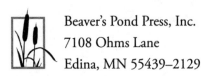

Beaver's Pond Press, Inc.
7108 Ohms Lane
Edina, MN 55439–2129

(952) 829-8818
www.BeaversPondPress.com

To Bill, Abby, Emily, and Alex

My wonderful family—you are always in my corner.

Contents

Prologue

April 2001—Abemly Shores, South Carolina

HER HAND FELT SO COLD AND FRAIL IN HIS as he watched her fade in and out of consciousness. Jonas prayed the sporadic up-and-down movements of her chest would become stronger and more regular. However, they only became more strained and shallow as the beautiful once-aspiring ballerina now lay in a contorted fetal position.

Jonas whispered in her ear, "Charlotte, you are my life, the mother of our child, my best friend, my wife. You can't leave me—can't leave us."

As tears welled in his eyes and spilled over onto her cheek, she woke.

"You mustn't be sad for me, my love. You know I'll always be here." She winced as she reached to touch his heart. "I promise you that. Just know I'll be watching over you and JJ and everyone I care so much for."

She closed her eyes and took a deep breath.

Jonas tightened his grip on her arm. "Charlotte! Wait!" He was almost shouting. "I love you so much. You will always be my beautiful ballerina. I'll never stop loving you." He gently took her emaciated body in his arms.

She drew yet another breath. Her eyes opened, searching his face.

"You have to promise you'll make a happy life for yourself and JJ. And there's one more thing, Jonas—you will find love and a forever mother for JJ. It may take time, but you'll recognize her when it's right. Please promise me this."

She smiled and squeezed his hand with the last bit of energy she could muster.

"Now please open the window so I can feel the breeze and take in the sweet smell of honeysuckle once more."

Jonas granted her last request, then lay down with her. They shared one last kiss as she took one last breath with love in her eyes and a smile on her lips.

At that moment, Jonas felt a cool, soothing breeze dance around them and a lingering scent of honeysuckle in the air.

Part
One

Chapter 1

THE PRESENCE

April 2001—Abemly Shores

EYES REDDENED AND BLURRY, Jonas drove back home. He needed to explain to a three-year-old why his mother would never come home again.

How the hell am I supposed to tell JJ his mother is gone forever? He's only a baby. He needs his mom.

Jonas wiped his eyes with the back of his hand.

Damn leukemia!

He glanced in the rearview mirror as the hospital, where he last held the love of his life, disappeared from sight.

What am I going to do without her? She was my rock, my life.

"Damn," he said aloud.

Jonas was now heading back to his in-laws' cottage, where they and his beautiful little boy waited. He just knew that when he turned the bend in the tree-lined road leading to the cottage, he would see the small boy standing on the front porch smiling and waving.

My son. A dagger pierced his heart.

Charlotte Sills and Jonas Beckman had grown up together, gone to school together, then became high school sweethearts. Jonas went off to a nearby college but came home every weekend to see Charlotte. She was following in her mother's footsteps, teaching piano. She also spent several hours a week in dance classes to perfect her ultimate passion for ballet. On the side, she worked at Jonas's Fine Café.

The café had been a local supermarket until the Beckman family purchased it just after Jonas was born. His father, Steve, was so elated to finally have a son after three daughters that he christened the café in Jonas's name. And because there were no "fine" food restaurants around, he decided the town needed Jonas's Fine Café.

All four Beckman children grew up working part time in the café. Eventually two of the girls went off to college, found husbands, and never moved back. Sylvie, the sister two years older than Jonas, married her high school sweetheart and opened a thriving grocery in a nearby town.

In the middle of Jonas's second year of college, he felt the pull to return home to the café—and most importantly to Charlotte. It was difficult for them to be apart. They were married in February 1996. It was unseasonably warm that year, so

6

they said their vows on the porch of the beach cottage Charlotte had grown up in. The elated wedding guests mingled among the gardens below.

Steve and Shelly Beckman retired early and moved to Naples, Florida, once they were comfortable with Jonas taking over his namesake café.

A little over a year into their marriage, Charlotte and Jonas found they were expecting a child. Jonas was concerned about the pregnancy because of Charlotte's waifish physique. So were Cecilia and John, Charlotte's parents. But she assured them of her toughness and that all would be fine.

Three days before their second wedding anniversary, they welcomed a son into the world. Jessup Jonas Beckman was named after his grandfather, Jonathon Jessup Sills, and his father, Jonas Steven Beckman. Everyone immediately began calling him JJ. He was so handsome and striking with all that black hair and his big dark eyes. The people in town always commented about the gorgeous little Beckman boy.

Jonas and Charlotte were truly living a storybook life. Even though money was tight, they were in love. They both worked hard at the café to make ends meet. Charlotte taught piano when her parents or Jonas could watch JJ for an hour or two. The three of them lived in a small apartment above the café and were extremely comfortable in their cozy little nest.

After the first few years, Charlotte began to constantly pick up colds or the flu from her students. It seemed all she had to do was be near anyone who was ill. Sadly, after seeing several doctors, Charlotte was diagnosed with leukemia.

As days turned to months, she became so weak that it was difficult for her to care for her family on her own. The three of them moved into her parents' home near the shore. Jonas and Charlotte stayed in the guest room on the first floor, as it was easier for Charlotte. JJ had the room his mother had grown up in, which was at the top of the stairs and next to his grandparents' room.

Growing weaker, Charlotte was forced to spend most of her time in bed. JJ loved playing in her room near the open window with the scent of honeysuckle and magnolia floating through the air. When she was able, she enjoyed lying on the chaise on the front porch covered up with the double-wedding-ring quilt her mother had made for her wedding. There, she would rest peacefully for hours, sometimes with her family and sometimes alone. She'd delight in the fragrance of the garden below and listen to the surf tease the shore.

On that same porch in early spring, when the flowers were starting to bloom and nature was coming alive, JJ was frozen in a photograph. He blew a kiss to his mother for her to hold until she returned home from the hospital.

But she never did.

As his car crept up Main Street, Jonas pictured a healthy Charlotte, without a care in the world, walking into Mona Argyle's Book Benders shop to pick up the newest romance novel. Charlotte always told him she had yet to read a romance that could ever compare to their own. Jonas blinked his tears away, smiled at that memory, and continued up the street.

He pulled the car to the curb in front of the café. He remembered when they had first been married and lived upstairs in the small apartment. He had carried Charlotte over the threshold. They had conceived a child there and brought him home to that place where love lived so bright and warm. He folded his arms over the steering wheel and lowered his head to cry.

When he lifted his head from arms now damp with tears, he saw Mona coming toward him with her dog, Josie, a curly white poodle with apricot markings. She tapped on his window.

"Are you all right in there? Jonas, open the window. Please talk to me."

He got out of the car. She took one look at him and knew immediately what had happened. He put his arms around her and sobbed. She in turn cradled him while he continued to repeat, "Charlotte, my Charlotte."

She dug into her purse and handed him a hankie, then brought him to sit on a nearby bench.

"I'm so sorry," she said with tears in her eyes. "Jonas, she was very sick and in so much pain. Even though we don't want to say goodbye, she's much more comfortable now. She can rest in peace."

He leaned over, crying and hugging his stomach, while Mona rubbed his back. Josie curled around his feet with a sorrowful moan.

After sitting in silence, Jonas took Mona's chin in his hand and kissed her cheek.

"Thank you so much for being here for me. I'll never forget it."

He bent down and gave Josie a hug. Josie of course appreciated it, but Jonas realized he did too.

"Nothing like the unconditional love of a four-legged animal to help you heal," he said. He nodded goodbye to Mona, got back in his car, and let it take him wherever it willed.

Soon he found himself parked facing the ocean. Jonas got out of the car and meandered down the beach. He stood in the exact spot where he had proposed to Charlotte so many years before.

What would his life be like now without her? How could he raise a three-year-old and fight through such pain and denial at the same time?

Jonas picked up a round, flat white stone. He rubbed its smooth surface between his fingers as he walked.

He looked to the sun without feeling its warmth. He walked barefoot among the waves without feeling the water. He sat on the beach and sifted sand through his hands without feeling its softness. Finally, he lay down and stared up at the sky without seeing.

He closed his eyes. The tears came. They kept flowing till he was too worn to shed another.

A soft breeze began to perform a gentle bourrée. The dance massaged his throbbing temples. Then suddenly the wind kicked up its dancing feet.

He felt! He felt the breeze doing glissades and pirouettes over his exhausted body. That scent riding on the wind—he could smell it! He knew it so well. It was then, in his mind's eye, that the wind began its dramatic, fragrant finale of this enchanted ballet.

Feeling totally spent yet relaxed, he ran his fingers through the sand. As he did, he saw he was still holding that white stone. Examining the stone as he sat up, he saw something in it that made him think of his broken heart. Across the center of the stone was a tiny imperfection in the form of a faded red zigzag.

He tossed it in the air, caught it on the fly, and closed his fist tightly around it.

Well, I'm as ready as I'll ever be to go to my son.

He stood and dusted off the sand. He began walking back up the beach to his car. Then he stopped to take one last look at the place in which he gave his heart away, asking the love of his life to marry him. He touched again the smooth stone between his fingers. He brought it to his lips, then tossed it into the great ocean.

"This is for you, my love. Sleep well."

As he turned toward the car, the wind did an encore, one final series of pirouettes, dancing a protective circle around him.

Chapter 2

BEGINNING AGAIN

Summer 2001—Abemly Shores

FATHER AND SON MOVED OUT OF THE COTTAGE and back to the apartment over Jonas's Fine Café, where the three of them had been so happy together, before Charlotte's sickness. JJ was pretty much Jonas's whole world now, and that was just how Jonas wanted it. He wanted nothing else and no one else in his life.

In the weeks after Charlotte's death, Jonas began to close himself off. He became a difficult guy to get to know or even talk to. Quiet and reserved, he gave off an attitude that he needed *no one.*

The days dragged on as Jonas tried to put their life back together. He tried to be patient when JJ would ask about his mother, when she would be coming home. But it was so difficult to hear those questions when Jonas was trying so hard to just get on with the day-to-day grind. It further closed himself off from his pain as well as from all who loved him.

Under it all, Jonas couldn't let go of the guilt—perhaps he could have done more, understood more about her condition. Perhaps he could have kept her alive longer. Of course, it wasn't his fault. Everyone tried to tell him that, particularly his in-laws and even little JJ.

Jonas often sent JJ to stay at the cottage near the beach. Jonas wouldn't stay any longer, though, than to drop JJ off and say a quick hello before heading out. The cottage still held too many memories of Charlotte's last days.

JJ loved being at the cottage, however. His grandparents adored him, as he did them. It was there that JJ felt content and so consumed with love that he rarely spoke about his mother in a sad way. Rather, when he spoke of her, he would say she was happy now.

"She loves dancing like the wind," he said, "in heaven."

"That is such a lovely thought, JJ," Grandma Cecilia said, smiling as she rocked and sang to him on the big porch.

It was summer now, and the days were getting hotter. The porch was a lovely place to sit early in the morning as the sun rose or in the late afternoon as the sun sank from the sky.

"Grandma, it's not just a thought! It's true!" JJ insisted, jumping off her lap very deliberately and placing his small hands on his waist. "Mama told me! She likes to dance like the wind!"

Rubbing his eyes, he ran from the porch to the flower garden, sat down, and cried.

During the day, JJ would go to the beach with Granddad John and Grandma Cecilia. They would play with the big beach

JUST SOMETHING IN THE WIND

ball or hold hands and run in the water till the waves chased them to shore.

Other times in the hot afternoons, they would sit in the living room and "make music," as JJ called it. Cecilia would sit at the piano and play a song from *The Music Man*. JJ would sit next to her and dance his fingers across the keys, making up his own accompaniment as he went along. John would pick up his French horn and join them.

"See, Cecilia—he loves music like his mother did!" John announced as he gave the boy a loving pat on the head.

As summer turned to fall, it was time for school and music lessons to begin. Cecilia worked at school in the mornings and taught piano most afternoons and evenings. John taught music at the school all day as well as gave private lessons at night. In other words, JJ couldn't spend time at the cottage during the weekdays; he would have to be with his dad at the café.

This posed a problem. Jonas loved his son dearly and enjoyed spending time with him, but he didn't really understand the ways of a three-year-old child. And while JJ had been happily occupied at the cottage all summer, Jonas had withdrawn even more. When not working at the café, he had spent nearly all his time alone and isolated. Charlotte was constantly in the forefront of his mind, as he was always reflecting on what his life could have—and should have—been.

Of course, JJ thought he was a big boy now. He wanted to help in the café. Certainly too young to cook and too small to bus tables, he took on the self-appointed job of greeting and entertaining guests coming through the door. The patrons loved the boy with dark eyes and dark hair. He was beginning to look a lot like a mini Jonas. The difference was that he was delightfully happy and pleasant to be around, unlike his father.

JJ was as happy and helpful as a small boy could be, but Jonas knew JJ needed to be around friends his own age. Jonas enrolled him in a preschool program. It was the best decision for JJ—and for Jonas himself.

JJ took to it right away. When he walked into the classroom, the first thing that caught his attention was the piano. Comfortable with adults as he was, he asked the teacher if there would be time for him to "make music" for the class. She was tickled by his question and suggested he perform during snack time. When snack time came, JJ was elated to entertain his classmates with a piece he'd learned from Grandma Cecilia. It was a familiar song. Several of the students clapped and sang along. He was quite the hit. Several of his classmates approached him at recess, asking if he would be their best friend.

Needless to say, when Jonas came to pick him up after school that first day, JJ wouldn't let him get a word in edgewise. He talked all the way home, through dinner, and up until it was time to climb into bed.

Before Jonas could kiss him good night, JJ threw his arms around him, looked in those eyes that mirrored his own, and said, "Daddy, I love you so much! Thank you for taking me to school." Then he gave him a big kiss on the cheek.

Jonas tried to hide the tears welling up in his eyes. He reciprocated the hug and tucked him in.

"Good night, JJ. I love you bunches!" Jonas said, kissing his son on the top of his head. He turned out the light and blew a kiss. "Sweet dreams, my big boy," he said softly as he made an attempt to hold back his tears until closing the door to JJ's room.

A memory hit him between the eyes of Charlotte leaning down to brush a lock of hair from their son's eyes just before granting him a good-night kiss. *Oh, what a beautiful family we were*, he thought to himself.

Then Jonas closed the door, mumbling under his breath, "Why were we chosen to be broken this way?" The tears came fast and furious. He wiped them away with the back of his hand. "It's time for me to be here as the best dad I can be. That's the way Charlotte would want it!"

Life settled into a routine, and time passed. When JJ's birthday rolled around in 2003, Jonas could hardly believe his little boy was already turning five. To mark the occasion, JJ's grandparents bought an electric piano just his size to have at the apartment. JJ loved making music on his very own piano, and sometimes he even pretended to come up with his own songs.

"Daddy, I want to play for the people at the café! Please?" he asked over and over again. "When can I play downstairs?"

One time, he followed this question by stomping his feet. "Mommy would let me!"

Jonas was shocked and angered by the statement. "And how, my son, do you know this?" It was all he could do to keep calm.

"She told me! Mommy talks to me sometimes," JJ announced as if it were an everyday occurrence. "She always has, since the day you took that picture of me blowing her a kiss on the porch, for her to have at the hospital."

Jonas sat down next to JJ. "We need to have a man-to-man talk here." Trying his hardest to be diplomatic, he continued, "How can you talk to your mother when she isn't here anymore?"

A tear dripped down JJ's cheek. "Daddy, I *do* talk to Mommy. She comes to be near me. She says she loves us very much but has to live in heaven. She says you need lots of hugs from me." On cue, the little boy gave his dad as big a hug as a five-year-old could. "She did also say I play my piano good and that people downstairs would like to hear me make music."

Jonas stared at JJ as the slightest smile spread across his face. He didn't know if JJ's words spoke of something truly spiritual or merely make-believe. Either way, it made Jonas feel better.

Jonas gave in just enough to allow the little piano to be moved into the café. After school or on the weekends, JJ played for the patrons of the café. Someone definitely had the right idea. The people totally enjoyed the entertainment, and JJ was thrilled to be doing something fun that he felt good about.

By the time summer rolled around again, he began taking "serious" piano lessons from Cecilia. They still spent time at the beach too. Sometimes Jonas would even join them. As time went on, Jonas was becoming more comfortable again at the little cottage near the shore. There were times he would sit in that cozy living room and listen to JJ and his grandparents play music. He'd even sing along. He also shared many Sunday dinners talking and laughing on that big front porch where he and Charlotte had wed.

Chapter 3

FOURTH OF JULY GRILL MASTERS

July 2003—Abemly Shores

By summer, John and Cecilia felt it was time to open their home to family and friends once again. With Jonas and JJ's help, they planned an informal Fourth of July party. Even Jonas was looking forward to entertaining and visiting.

JJ was so excited, he could barely stop chattering. "Daddy, can I have my friends come to our party? And my teacher too? And is Aunt Sylvie coming with Brett and Marshall? They're only four and I'm five, but I like to play with them anyway. Sometimes they try to trick me and make me guess who they are, like it's a game, just because they're twins. But I'm a whole year older than they are, and I'm pretty smart, so I can always tell who's who. We have lots of fun together playing tag and building forts."

"Sure," Jonas said when JJ took a breath. "They can all come to our party! Are you going to be my assistant grill master? It's a very important job, you know. We'll be responsible for feeding all the guests and making sure they have a good time."

JJ stared at his dad admiringly. "Wow, that sounds like a big-boy job! Yeah, Dad, I'll help you make food and feed all our friends. I'll probably have to help Brett and Marshall dish up their food 'cuz they're still pretty young. I'm so excited they can come! It'll almost be like having brothers of my own to take care of and help them do stuff." Without a pause, JJ asked, "When will I have a real brother, huh, Dad? They're brothers. They have each other."

Considering Jonas had not dated since he lost Charlotte and had no thoughts of remarrying, ever, he attempted to change the subject. "You and your cousins can be in charge of the other children when we start the fireworks. You have to make sure they don't get too close because it can be very dangerous."

"Well, okay. I am pretty good at being a boss. I guess I can be the boss of the other kids." He let out a confident sigh as he perched the backs of his hands on his hips. "What color fireworks will we have, Dad?"

"I'm not sure about specific colors. But no matter what, they'll be really cool and very special because we'll be at the cottage with everyone we care about."

"Not everyone we care about. Mommy won't be there." JJ looked down at his feet and kicked at the dirt.

Jonas squatted down in front of JJ, took his hands, and gave them a delicate shake. "I miss her too, buddy. But as you always tell me, she'll be here in spirit watching over us." Then he picked JJ up, squeezed him, and held him close.

The day of the party began with the sun showing its warm face through Jonas's window. He could sense the light trying to force open his sleeping eyelids. It was the lovely, familiar breeze, however, that finally managed to open them.

"Ah, good morning, my love." He smiled as he caressed the gentle face of the woman in the photo on his nightstand. "We're doing well these days, your son and I. We're having a Fourth of July party at the cottage, but you probably already know that." He wished he could actually speak to her. "JJ is so happy to help me fix the food, and he's excited to take care of his cousins. But he wishes he had a brother of his own." Rubbing the sleep out of his eyes, he continued, "I just don't know how to tell him there won't be brothers or sisters. For that matter, there will only be him and me!"

Suddenly the morning breeze let loose a swirling gust through the window, knocking over the photo. Jonas caught it before it hit the floor.

A little unnerved, he jumped out of bed, stretched, and ran his hands briefly through his disheveled hair. He tossed the blanket over the mattress, attempting to imitate a made bed. Jonas then walked to the window and took a deep breath of the warm morning air.

It's a new day, he thought, *and I'll treat it so.*

Heading to the shower, he paused at the next room to peek at his sleeping son. Again, a sigh came from Jonas, but this time a content one. He smiled and just shook his head as he walked across the hall to the bathroom.

What a great kid I have, and what a lucky guy I am.

Once out of the shower and refreshed, Jonas stood at the bathroom mirror with only a towel wrapped around his waist. Just as he lifted his razor, he heard a little knock on the door.

"Come in if you are a grill master. Otherwise, be on your way!"

"It's me, Dad. And I'm an assistant grill master . . . is that okay?" Sounding a bit confused, JJ waited for the answer before walking in.

"Well, that sounds perfect. You may enter."

Jonas tried to look very serious, but he was chuckling on the inside as he gazed at JJ through the mirror.

"Are you all ready for our big party today?" Jonas asked.

"Yep, I sure am. I'm going to be a good 'almost' big brother to my cousins too."

Watching his dad shave was the best, so he took a seat and watched in awe as the stubble disappeared.

"Shaving is really cool. Will I be able to do that soon?"

Jonas tried to control his laughter so as not to insult the boy. "Soon enough, son, but don't be in a hurry to grow up just yet. It's so much fun being a kid. Enjoy it now while you can!"

He set the razor down on the sink and gave JJ a hug and a big shaving-cream kiss on the cheek.

"Oops! I guess you'll have to take a shower now, big guy!"

"Aw, thanks a lot, Dad!" He giggled and tried to wipe his face clean with a towel. "Well, since it's the party day, I guess I can shower."

"Well, then, better hop in, buddy. We've gotta get a move on!"

"Okay, Dad. And Dad? I love you!"

JJ, clad in his grilling apron, stood at attention before Jonas with a big grin on his face.

"Dad, this is a fun party. I like the Fourth of July! When do the fireworks start?"

Cecilia watched them from the porch. She smiled as she shook out the double-wedding-ring quilt, lovingly folded it, then placed it back on the chaise. She walked down the steps to John, who was talking to Mona Argyle. She nodded and gave him a kiss, then continued over to the grilling station to check on her boys.

The day was hot and humid, but a lovely breeze was coming from the ocean. It played with Cecilia's short curls. She gave her head a shake from the tickle.

"How's it going, boys?" She mussed JJ's hair and gave Jonas a light kiss on the cheek. "Thanks for coming," she whispered to Jonas. "This is special for all of us."

"We're doing great, Grandma!" JJ replied. "The burgers and hot dogs will be the best ever!"

He looked to Jonas for approval. Jonas winked and smiled.

"Dad and I are good grillers when we work together! Right, Dad?"

"That's absolutely correct, JJ. We make a great team, you and I!"

John walked up behind them and put his arms around Jonas and JJ.

"How are my guys? Looks like you've got this under control. But if you need any help, remember I can flip a burger as well as any of them!" He chuckled and gave JJ a high five.

Cecilia hooked her arm through John's and smiled. "John, I think the Beckman men can take care of the grilling without your help. Time to be gracious hosts to our guests."

Walking away, she peeked back at the grill and caught Jonas holding JJ's hand with the spatula, teaching him to flip a burger. JJ had a very serious look on his face that changed to an ear-to-ear grin as the burger flipped over in the air and landed on its other side.

JJ was so happy and proud of his accomplishment that he didn't think the day could get any better. But it did! His cousins told him he was the best "almost" big brother and that they never had a burger that tasted as good.

Then his "almost" brothers asked him to please sit between them during the fireworks 'cuz they were kind of scared and he was bigger and made them feel safe. The three of them sat under the stars on that warm night in July, watching the colorful explosions dance across the sky. The ocean breeze sashayed lightly and watched over them and all the guests at the Sillses' cottage.

Chapter 4

COUSINS

August 2003—Abemly Shores

AFTER THAT SPECIAL FOURTH OF JULY when JJ became honorary big brother to his cousins, Brett and Marshall, he spent much of the summer playing with them. They enjoyed the hot and muggy days at the Sillses' cottage, playing on the beach and running through the waves with Grandpa John and Grandma Cecilia. (John and Cecilia were more than happy to be honorary grandparents. As they saw it, Jonas was family, and by extension, so was his sister Sylvie and her family.) Sometimes JJ even helped his cousins learn a few elementary songs on the grand piano, with its view of the ocean and the constant friendly breeze dancing through the open windows.

Other times, the three boys played at Aunt Sylvie and Uncle Nathan's house. Nathan shared his love of fishing with the boys when he could take time away from the grocery store they owned and operated.

It was a hot August day, and JJ was fishing with the boys. Suddenly, he had to struggle just to hang on to his pole.

"Uncle Nate! I think I have a bite!" The line jumped and tugged, but he wouldn't let go.

Laughing excitedly, Brett and Marshall ran back and forth along the shore of the little lake. "Hold on, JJ! Don't let go! Don't let go!"

The small boys screamed with delight as their dad took JJ's hand and helped reel in the fish. When they saw the wiggling fish on the line, all three boys squealed and began jumping around, giving high fives.

Fishing was so good that they produced a plentiful fish dinner. Jonas and Sylvie joined in for the fun, deciding to pitch tents in the backyard and put the grill masters to work.

"This is so cool!" Brett said.

"Can we cook marshmallows over the fire? Maybe we can even sit around the campfire and tell ghost stories," Marshall chimed in.

JJ looked to Jonas with a little worry. "Ah . . . I don't know about ghost stories. I kind of . . . um . . . Dad?"

JJ motioned with a finger that he needed to talk to Jonas privately.

"Dad," he whispered, "you know I'm a little weird about ghost stories. So, can you kind of help with this?" JJ gulped and gave his dad a crooked little smile.

Jonas nodded and gave his son a knowing smile with a bit of sadness behind those large dark eyes. "I think ghost stories is a great idea," he announced to the group, "as long as the stories aren't *too* spooky!"

Just then, he roared like a lion and grabbed the two cousins from behind. With one in each arm, he swung them around. Then he put them down to chase after JJ, who was laughing and trying to run away. Jonas caught him in a bear hug, picked him up, and spun him around too.

"Dad!" JJ yelled in between hysterical giggles. "Let me down! I'm getting dizzy! I might even throw up on you!"

Jonas planted a big kiss on JJ, gave him one more squeeze, then set him down. JJ ran off to the house to help the other boys collect the important things for the campout, such as sleeping bags and marshmallows.

"I better help the campers with their gear," Sylvie said as she gave Nate a kiss.

She took a few steps, then turned and squeezed her brother's hand. "You know," she said quietly, "JJ does need a mother figure—and a female companion for you wouldn't hurt."

She flashed a sly smile, nodded to Nate, then headed into the house.

Jonas watched her go before he glanced over at his brother-in-law. "I know what you're going to say—don't." He threw his hands up in the air and brought them down to slap at his thighs. "I'm sorry. It's just a difficult subject for me, you know?"

Now rubbing his thighs with the palms of his hands, Jonas leaned over, looking down at the campfire-in-waiting.

"Charlotte was the one, the only one. I know it's been a while, but to me, it feels like only yesterday when I kissed her goodbye." He squatted at the fire pit and began haphazardly arranging the firewood. He shook his head. "I understand life has to go on—our lives have to continue. But I don't even know where to begin. What am I supposed to do, bro?"

Nate sat down next to him. "It's okay to date now and then or at least go out for coffee and conversation. Hey, do you remember Donny Sands from high school? Well, his cousin just moved to town a little bit ago and doesn't know too many people. Her name is Cassie, and she's a columnist for the Abemly Shores paper. Sylvie has hung out with her some. She says Cassie's really nice but kind of quiet. She likes to keep to herself and almost seems sad. She doesn't say much about her life before Abemly. She's really into her work."

Nate tossed a few pieces of kindling on the fire.

"Maybe sometime you and Cassie could tear yourselves away from work, and the four of us could grab a pizza or something. I'm not pushing you to marry her. It's just a little friendship and adult conversation. Cassie could use it, and so could you."

Nate tried not to glance in his brother-in-law's direction, yet he could still feel uneasiness emanating from Jonas.

Jonas gave Nate a shake of the head and a pensive frown, then he stood up and dusted off the wood chips from his knees.

"I really appreciate what you and Syl are trying to do for me." He took a deep breath. "Okay. What could it hurt? I'll see when I can arrange a couple of hours off from the café. Now we better get going on those tents, so they're ready when the boys come back out." He turned to gather the tent poles, stopped, and looked back at his brother-in-law. "Thanks, bro."

Just as the men finished putting up the tents, they heard excited voices coming their way. The twins were quite a sight. Decked out in matching pj's, each boy carried a blankie over his shoulder, hugged a pillow and favorite stuffed animal under one arm, and dragged a sleeping bag in the other. JJ was pulling a wagon filled with hot dogs, condiments, buns, marshmallows, and two jugs of lemonade. Sylvie followed with foil to cook the fish plus the makings for hot chocolate and s'mores.

"This will be the coolest overnight ever!" Marshall said, giving his brother and cousin high fives. The boys grabbed their sleeping bags and bolted into the tent.

"How are you big boys getting along out here?" Sylvie asked the men. "Looks like it'll be a great fire and a beautiful night. Just look at those stars! Mmm! It smells so good. There's just a faint breeze to help ward off the bugs. But just in case . . . ta-da!" Sylvie held up bug spray.

Nate came up behind her and put his head on her shoulder. "We're on for a pizza night," he whispered, nodding toward Jonas. "Now you just need to talk to Cassie."

She turned and kissed him on the cheek. Grinning and humming, she went to plant a kiss on her brother. She took his face in her hands.

"It will be fine. You'll see. We'll have a nice time. And guess what? She doesn't bite!"

The campout was a great success. They ate until they would burst—then ate a little more. (Or should that be *s'more?*) Afterward, they told ghost stories—or "fireside tales," as JJ and Jonas called them—late into the night. They even sang a few songs. Right before turning in, Sylvie heated up the hot chocolate and dropped peppermint sticks into each mug. Then, of course, she added marshmallows in quantity.

Once tucked into their bags and tents, the boys fell fast asleep. Nate and Sylvie took the tent next to the boys.

Jonas stirred the fire until it was a mass of glowing embers, then slipped into his sleeping bag and stretched out with his hands behind his head. Gazing up at the stars and taking in the heady aroma of the fading smoke, he thought of his life and the special people in it.

Just then, the breeze picked up and danced over and around him. Smiling, he blew a kiss to the stars and drifted off to sleep. In his dreams, he and JJ danced in the wind . . . with the wind.

Chapter 5

MOVING ON

September 2003—Abemly Shores

THE WEEKS PASSED BY, AND AUGUST FLOWED into September. School began, and JJ was busy with the excitement of new friends and teachers. Jonas was preoccupied with creating the new fall menu at the café. John and Cecilia had gone back to teaching and working at school. Nate and Sylvie's grocery store was thriving, and Marshall and Brett were very excited about being big boys in 4K preschool.

Sylvie, however, still had enough time to think about matching up her brother with Cassie Sands—at least for one date. She gave Jonas a call.

"Hey, Sylvie. How are you?" Jonas said, picking up his cell. "What's up?"

"Hi there, little brother. I haven't heard from you since school started. I just wanted to touch base." She took a breath. "Remember the night of our campout with the kids? Remember how we talked about you getting together with my friend Cassie Sands?"

Jonas sighed and took a deep breath of his own. "Ah, yeah. I do recall a brief conversation along those lines, sis. But I'm really focused on getting the fall menu underway. I'm not sure it's a great time to start with something new."

"Um, excuse me?" Sylvie said. "That 'something new' is actually *someone* new. Plus, you already said you'd give this a try. Cassie is a workaholic at the paper, but she's agreed to drag herself away from her computer for one night. I just happen to know that she's free tomorrow. So it's a date. No ifs, ands, or buts. Come on, Jonas. You know you could use a night out. You may even enjoy yourself—novel idea!" She laughed lovingly as she hung up.

The following evening, JJ watched carefully as Jonas readied himself in front of the bathroom mirror. Trying to make his hair look as natural as possible, Jonas actually ended up overdoing it, causing a giant cowlick dead center.

"Oh man! Talk about a bad hair day!"

He quickly ran his hands under the water, rewet his hair, and began again. Spotting JJ through the mirror, he noticed his son awkwardly motioning to the side of his jaw. When Jonas examined his own jaw, he saw a smear of green toothpaste rapidly drying along his cheek.

"Oh man!" he said as he rubbed it off with his damp hand, then went back to working on his hair.

"Ah, Dad?" JJ began. "You said 'oh man' two times. And I hate to tell you, but now there's some green in your hair." With a serious look but also a little twinkle in his eye, he said, "Dad, are you sure you'll be okay going on a date alone? Do you want me to come with you, so you're not scared?"

Jonas grinned and mussed up JJ's hair. "To tell the truth, I might feel safer with you in my corner, buddy."

Then Jonas sat down on the side of the tub, held his son's elbows, and looked him straight in the eyes.

"I don't want you to think I'm trying to replace Mommy, because I could never do that. I will always love her."

"Me too!" JJ said. "I love Mommy, and she loves us! She wants us to be happy. She says there's a special lady that will be with us someday and love us always. Maybe Cassie is that lady," JJ said holding back tears and trying to smile.

"Whoa, buddy. First of all, Cassie's just a friend of Aunt Sylvie's. The four of us are just going to a football game and out for pizza after. No big deal. Second, what makes you think Mommy feels that way? Are you having dreams about her again?"

A tear escaped down JJ's cheek, and he pulled away from his dad. "I told you Mommy talks to me. I'm not always sleeping when she dances around me and tells me things like we'll have a family again and I'll have a new mommy who will love me very much and never have to leave me. Don't you believe me?"

Dropping down on his knees, Jonas took JJ in his arms and held him tight. "I'm sorry, JJ. I didn't mean to upset you. I know how you feel. Sometimes I sense she's close and watching over us." He sighed. "And who knows what the future may bring as far as a female in our lives. But for now, I'm going to take you to Grandma and Grandpa Sills's cottage. Brett and Marshall will be there too tonight."

JJ hugged him back and gave his dad a big sloppy kiss. "I'm glad you're not scared to go out with a girl without me, Dad, 'cuz I'm really excited to stay with Brett and Marshall at Grandma and Grandpa's house tonight. I can count the stars when I'm there because the sky is so clear. And I can listen to the ocean move back and forth while I fall asleep. I'm never afraid because the wind always dances around me and tickles my eyelashes—like butterfly kisses."

Cassie and Jonas had a nice time that evening. They enjoyed each other's company. The fact that the home team won that night was certainly a plus, keeping everyone excited and rooting. There were several high fives and toasts shared during the final moments of the game.

It was a lovely night, so the four of them next walked along Abemly Sound to the pizza place for a late dinner. To his surprise, Jonas was immersed in the warmth of the new friendship—until they neared the water. He became rather quiet as the wind kicked up, tossing familiar scents in the air.

All in all, though, the night was lovely. A friendship began to bloom between Jonas and Cassie. In fact, they continued to spend time together throughout the fall. They became good friends catching a movie, enjoying an occasional dinner, or just taking walks and sharing stories.

In the back of his mind, though, Jonas kept thinking about what JJ had said. He wondered if some woman really would come into his life and if Cassie Sands were the one. Still, he would take his time. He sensed Cassie was holding something back whenever he asked about her life. This—and the sensation of something yet to come, something in the wind—made it rather uncomfortable for Jonas to build the friendship into anything more.

One day as Christmas approached, Sylvie invited Jonas over for coffee. He knew what was coming.

"So," Sylvie asked, her eyes twinkling, "how's it going with you and Cassie?"

"Syl, I really like Cassie, and we enjoy spending time together. But I think there's something she's keeping from me, from all of us, about her past. She just clams up whenever I ask about it. Does she ever open up to you? She said she used to live in Philadelphia and was married. Does she ever talk about her ex-husband? Hell, I don't even know if he is her ex. For all I know, they're still married."

He took another cookie from the platter she had set down in the middle of the table.

"You still make the best molasses cookies, sis. Hands down. You could win prizes!"

He held up his coffee mug to toast her. She topped it off with more coffee and a big grin.

"No, she really hasn't said much about him," Sylvie said. "I don't ask either because I hate to grill her on a subject that seems painful. I figure she'll tell us about him when she's ready." She grabbed his chin and gave him a kiss on the cheek. "Have I ever told you how adorable you are and that you are my favorite brother?"

"Hmm . . . I'm your only brother," he said, tilting his head and questioning her motives.

Laughing, she said, "I know, but you're still the best, and I love you."

He shrugged and smiled while sneaking a few more cookies.

Chapter 6

CASSIE'S STORY

1984—Pennsylvania

GROWING UP IN A SMALL TOWN IN PENNSYLVANIA, Cassie had always loved reading and writing. She felt it was her great getaway and escape from the reality of her family life. Her parents had married young. They were high school sweethearts, and Cindy, her mom, had gotten pregnant during her senior year. It wasn't a good start to a solid family life.

At a young age, Cassie would carry her dolls, books, and a writing binder in either a wagon or a sled (depending on the time of year), and she'd escape to the small greenhouse behind her parents' modest home. The petite blond-haired, blue-eyed child read to those dolls and wrote for them as though they were children in a classroom. She loved this make-believe life. She kept her cherished secret school to herself. When Cassie was in the greenhouse, she could pretend there was happiness and love in her home, not yelling and crying, which happened all too frequently—especially when her dad, Dan, drank too much.

When Cindy finally couldn't take it anymore, she issued an ultimatum, and Dan went into a rehab program. He did well for six months, then began drinking again. This time, he would become even angrier. Sometimes Cassie would hear him tell Cindy it was her fault they had to marry. Cassie would run and hide in her safe place.

One particular day, Cassie was in the greenhouse when Cindy came in to find her.

"Honey?" she said, kneeling down before Cassie. "I have something very important to tell you. Your father is leaving." Her voice cracked, then she cleared her throat and swallowed, looking directly into her daughter's questioning eyes. "But it's going to be okay. It will be better this way, actually."

Crying and holding each other, Cassie and Cindy realized they'd have to make a new beginning. Their lives had to get better!

They grew closer and spent a lot more time together, often in the greenhouse, as Cindy was working toward starting a floral business. Cassie studied or read aloud to her mom while she worked. They talked about dreams they had and places they wanted to see. Cassie shared that she wanted to go to college, become a famous writer, and share her stories with readers all over the world. Cindy would smile and encourage her daughter to carry out her dreams.

The day finally came in 1995, when Cassie followed her dream all the way to Philadelphia. The petite blond-haired, blue-eyed eighteen-year-old gave her mom a kiss and a tearful hug, then walked confidently toward her college dormitory.

Cassie's freshman English class was great. Specifically, Charlie Tanum, the grad-student TA, was great—or at least that was what the other female students thought. He was smart, pleasant, and always ready to help students (particularly the females).

And he was downright gorgeous. Being a competitive swimmer for most of his life, he was six-pack lean and six feet tall. His sandy brown hair had enough wave to continuously fall across his twinkling emerald eyes. He'd give his head a slight but sexy shake, attempting to sweep away the hair, but it would immediately fall again.

The girls swooned to be first in line for his help. They'd be starry-eyed listening to his explanations, hanging on to every word spoken through his rugged Texas drawl. A bolo tie was part of his signature attire along with a suede blazer the color of a well-worn saddle and, of course, cowboy boots.

What a ladies' man he was with that comfortable "I like everyone" kind of personality. Even the male students and profs alike enjoyed his company.

Yes, Charlie was great. Well, that's what everyone but Cassie thought! She, on the other hand, went out of her way to avoid needing his help. Of course, this only fueled Charlie's interest in her. He tried to be extra charming and complimentary to her.

One day as Cassie was leaving English class with her arms full of books, Charlie sauntered up and deliberately swerved in front of her.

"Excuse me, Mizz Sands?" he asked. "You don't like me much, do ya, ma'am?"

Cassie let out an exasperated sigh. "Why would you call me ma'am? I'm not a 'ma'am' nor a 'Mizz Sands,'" she said, echoing his drawl. "My name is Cassie. And I'd appreciate it if you'd move out of my way so I can get to the library to work on my paper!"

She almost stomped her foot to show her annoyance, all the while trying not to look into those amazing green eyes that seemed to draw her into a hypnotic state.

"Mizz Sands—ah, I mean, Cassie—I'd be much obliged if you'd let me help you get started on that paper. After all, that's what I'm supposed to do as a teaching assistant. And if you're afraid to be alone with me, well, you don't need to worry. We'd be at the library with half the school."

Charlie reached to help her with her books, winking with a crooked little smirk.

Cassie pulled away so quickly, a pen slipped out of her armload. She put her nose in the air and looked straight into those dangerous eyes. "Mr. Tanum, I am perfectly capable of carrying my own books, and I'm certainly able to put together a paper without any help from the likes of you! But thank you *so* much for the thought," she said, batting her eyelashes and showing her own little smirk. "I am most certain there are other girls in the class who would cherish your coming to their aid."

At that, she gave him a sideways glance, excused herself, made her way past him, and huffed off to the library.

Charlie knelt down to pick up the pen she had dropped. Down on one knee, he rolled the pen in his fingers as he watched her climb the library steps. *Yes, ma'am . . . I think I'm in love!* he said to himself. Walking back into the building, he tapped the pen against the stubble outlining his rugged jawline.

The more she pushed him away, the more exciting she was to Charlie. She was like no other girl he had ever met. He loved her spunk. He decided that little blond-haired, blue-eyed, feisty bundle of energy would be his wife.

Yes, indeed!

Climbing the majestic library stairs, Cassie didn't even realize she was talking out loud to herself.

"That self-centered, egotistical womanizer, Mr. Charles Tanum, believes he can just worm his way into my good graces! Well, he's got another thing coming!"

She stomped into the library and let the heavily ornamented door slam behind her. Then she jumped when the sound exploded through the silence inside. Until she burst in, the only sound had been pages turning and computer keys clicking. A few people looked up at her in disgust.

Cassie tucked a blond strand of hair nervously behind her ear and looked at the floor as she scurried off to find a secluded place in the stacks. She sat down to start writing her paper. But she knew it'd take some time before she could think about anything other than that Charles Tanum.

The semester came to an end. Cassie had managed not only to pull a 4.0 in all eighteen credits but also to keep Mr. Tanum at arm's length. And by the way—she did just fine on the paper Charlie had wanted to help with. It turned out to be the top paper of the class. Her professor entered it in a competition, and it was printed as an article in the Philly city paper.

It was the beginning of winter break, and Cassie was looking forward to time with her mom and friends back home.

She was also excited about being able to spend her time doing nothing but writing if she so chose.

Zipping up her suitcase and hoisting it off the bed, she proudly slid a copy of the newspaper with her article into the front pocket. She pulled it out to take one last look at her name in print before tucking it away again.

I can't wait till Mom sees this—she'll be so excited, she thought. *And I didn't need a wink of help from you, Mr. Charlie Tanum—or any guy, for that matter!*

She placed her purse and computer bag over the handle of the overstuffed suitcase, flipped off the light in her dorm room, let the door lock behind her, then set off for a well-deserved vacation break.

After entering the scores in the computer, Charlie placed the last of the test papers in a folder and locked them in a file drawer. He walked over to check the cactus in his window. He put his finger in the soil to feel for dampness, then he glanced out the window just in time to see Cassie dragging a suitcase almost as big as her down the stairs and to the bus stop. He chuckled to himself as he saw the confidence in her walk and the determination in her eyes.

There you are—as smug as a bug in a rug! But Little Darlin', you wait and see. There'll be a time when I'm gonna look into those big blue eyes of yours and hear you say "I do!" Yep, just mark my words.

Charlie picked up his briefcase, then grabbed his suede blazer from the coatrack and swung it over his shoulder. He gave one more look toward the window with a smirk and a nod.

"See ya next year, Little Darlin'!" he said out loud.

Chapter 7

SHE LOVES ME, SHE LOVES ME NOT

1996—Pennsylvania

BACK AT SCHOOL BEFORE SHE KNEW IT, Cassie was again hard at work to make the grade and to constantly strive for the prize at the end of the tunnel: her writing career. She was briskly walking across campus, hoping to warm up with a quick chai at the Stop 'n' Drop Café, when she realized there was a crunching in the snow coming closer and moving up on her left.

"Hey there, Lit—I mean, Cassie," he said, tipping his Stetson to her.

Cassie didn't say a word to him. But she had a lot to say to herself.

That silly, egotistical Texan is always two-steppin' around wherever I am! I'm sure he means well. He's polite enough. And those eyes! She had to catch herself. *But I have an agenda, and it doesn't include him. There are plenty of girls looking his way. Why won't he leave me alone?*

"How's the writing going?" Charlie continued as he followed her. "I sure do miss having you in class this semester. How was your winter break? Mine was, well, pretty nice. I went back to the great state of Texas to spend time with my family. Even got some ridin' in."

Cassie kept walking in silence.

"I see you're headed to the café. Well, now, isn't that something? Me too! So are you gonna let me buy you a cup of coffee or something to take the chill out of those little bones of yours?"

Now Cassie just stopped and stared at him in amazement. "Oh my word. Are you kidding me? Do you ever get tired of hearing yourself talk, Mr. Tanum?"

"That's Charlie to you, now that you aren't a student in my class," he said with that sexy, toothy grin. He brushed off a pine needle that had landed on her coat. "Aw, come on. It's freezing out here. Let's at least get into the warmth, then talk this over."

She sighed, feeling like a bull giving up to its rider. "Fine! I can't believe I'm going anywhere with you, but it's only in hopes that you will finally let up on me."

In one of life's little twists, what Cassie assumed would be a dreadful time was quite the opposite. It turned out they had lots to talk about and even some things in common.

Charlie had always wanted to be a writer. However, he decided to finish his master's degree first. He was working his way through school as a TA in the English department. He also played guitar and sang in a local pub. With that money as a cushion, he searched out publications to write for and had plans to perhaps even put a novel together.

They talked about their childhoods and wishes and dreams. They shared laughter and woes. At last they glanced out the window, and it was dark.

"Wow, I can't believe we sat here talking this long!" Cassie said. Then she added with a laugh, "And you didn't even have to hold me against my will! I really better get back to the dorm, or I'll miss dinner altogether."

Charlie leaned across the table and reached for her hand. "Cassie, please let me take you out to dinner. We won't go far. There's actually a grill in walking distance. It has great soups and burgers. I promise I'll be a gentleman and get you home before you turn into a pumpkin," he said, grinning that grin he'd hoped she was getting comfortable with.

"I suppose we do both have to eat. What could it hurt? Two out-of-work writers having a bite together on a cold, wintry night." She smiled back at him and tapped her hand on his.

Charlie politely helped her with her coat and picked up her stack of books. "Is it all right if I carry your books for you now?"

"Well, I guess I'll allow it—but just this time." She giggled while she stretched her hat over her head.

After dinner, Charlie walked Cassie back to her dorm. First he held her gloved hand in his. Then when she began shivering from the cold, he put his arm around her until they reached the door. Finally, he turned her to face him and pulled up her coat collar to keep the harsh wind from burning her skin. He gently took her chin in his hand. Speaking without words, he kissed her gently. His twinkling green eyes connected with her big baby-blues to gauge her reaction. Cassie very slowly but deliberately lifted her hand to rub against his cheek, then followed it with another soft kiss.

"Thank you for dinner. I had a wonderful time. And thank you for finding me tonight and helping me discover you."

She took her books from him and set them on the stoop. Looking up at him with those blue eyes that drove him wild, she reached up to slide her arms around his neck.

"Kiss me again, but *really* kiss me this time, Charlie."

His arms engulfed her while his lips seemed to feed off hers. There they stood out in the winter wind, feeling only the warmth between them as they made wordless promises they hoped to keep.

"You should head in, Cassie," Charlie said, as much as he hated to let her go. "You'll freeze out here in the cold."

"Only if you promise we'll see each other tomorrow."

Charlie reluctantly let go of her and picked up the books for her. "Tomorrow, then, Little Darlin'."

He searched her face to see if she minded the endearing name he had secretly been calling her for months now.

She blushed and smiled, then gave him another peck on the cheek. "Good night and sleep well."

Opening the door with her key card, she took one last peek to watch him saunter off to his car. She sighed. Warm shivers began in her stomach, then tickled right up her arms and into her shoulders. She crossed her arms and gave herself a hug. What an exquisite way to end the evening. She touched her lips and giggled, thinking of him and the name he had bestowed on her . . . Little Darlin'.

The days and weeks following were a dream come true. The new couple was evolving into something neither of them would have dreamed. They tried to see each other at least once a day—even if it was just a short walk to class or a quick meeting at the Stop 'n' Drop to pick up coffees on the go. No matter what, though, they always spoke on the phone before closing their eyes at night and shutting out whatever issues they had encountered during the day.

As enamored with each other as they were, they never did more than kiss. Cassie knew she wasn't ready to share her bed with him yet. It wasn't a problem about not being attracted to him. Actually, Cassie was head over heels for him and could feel the passion between them.

Rather, it all stemmed from her parents' history. Having to get married so young because of an unplanned pregnancy eventually destroyed their happiness and family. She knew she and Charlie would be careful to prevent pregnancy, but one just never knows.

Thankfully, Charlie completely understood her nervousness.

"Little Darlin', as much as I'd love for us to be . . . well, more intimate with each other . . . I can wait until the time is right. As long as I can hold you in my arms while looking into those beautiful blue eyes of yours—yes, I can wait. Cassie, you must know how precious you are to me and how important 'we' are now and always have been for me."

Taking her hands in his, Charlie added, "I love you and can't imagine being with any other woman in my lifetime." He brought her hands to his lips, kissing them.

She looked up at him as a tear trickled down her face. "Charlie, I can't tell you how many times my head fought with my heart those first few months after we met. What I mean is,

Mr. Tanum, you were such a ninny, driving me crazy!" Laughing through her tears, she snorted, "Until my heart won out and my head followed. Charlie, I love you so much!"

She took his head in her hands and placed a loving kiss on his lips, muffling his words back to her. They stopped to look at each other with love and happiness in their eyes, then they shared a passionate kiss.

Summer was fast approaching. The flowers were quickly making their debut, and the campus green space was getting greener and more populated with students. Often, Charlie and Cassie would meet at the green space around lunchtime, bringing picnic food and whatever work they needed to finish.

During one of these picnics, Charlie lay on his side with one hand propping up his head and the other strumming the cool grass. He looked up at Cassie. "Hey, Little Darlin', you know I have to go back home for a while this summer to help Dad on the ranch. He just can't do it all anymore since he had that bad fall and messed up his back. I'd love for you to come out and meet the fam. Mom, Dad, and Rich would love to finally meet the goddess I've been raving about. You might even get a chance to hear me sing ya a little love song when Rich and I play at his bar."

He pushed himself up into a sitting position with legs crossed, pretending to strum an invisible guitar and gazing deep into her ocean-blue eyes.

"Little Darlin', my Little Darlin'," he sang.

Cassie pushed him over. As he fell to his back, he reached out to take her with him.

She laughed. "There you go again, talking a blue streak!"

He wrapped his arms around her, but before he could get close enough for a kiss, she playfully moved her head.

"Why, Mr. Tanum—we're surrounded by people on a public campus. I wouldn't want you to get arrested for PDA in the first degree!"

"What are you talkin' about, public display of affection? They ain't seen nothin' yet."

He gave her a big, loud, sloppy kiss—which did get a few heads turning.

Taunting him, she did her best Southern drawl. "Why, sir, you embarrass me!" She fanned herself with a half-eaten ham sandwich, fluttered her eyelashes, and turned away from him. "Besides, is that any way for an English scholar to speak? Hmm? 'They ain't seen nothin' yet'?"

They laughed together, and she smiled softly.

"On a more serious note, you know I can't come to Texas till the end of the summer." She took his hand, massaging his fingers. "You know I'm studying in England for a month, then meeting up with my mom to travel through France and visit with long-lost relatives in Lyon."

Charlie sighed. "I know, but I keep hoping those plans will all go away, and you'll just come and stay with me all summer. A guy can dream, can't he?" He placed kisses along the palm of her hand and looked up at her with puppy dog eyes. "It'll be a long couple of months, Little Darlin'."

"I'm sorry. But just think how special it'll be when we are together again. And maybe"—she touched his shoulder, having a difficult time getting the words out—"maybe after we've had time apart, I'll be ready to take the next step."

A nervous little smile came across her face as she bit her lip between her teeth and took a peek toward him to see his reaction.

Charlie got to his feet and took her hands to pull her up too. He leaned in to whisper, "I'm already the luckiest guy in the world to have you in my life. But wow—I don't know what to say except, let's get summer rollin' on!"

The lovebirds did make it through the summer. The night they returned to campus, Cassie helped Charlie unpack his suitcase at his apartment. She kept glancing uneasily at his bed.

"I'm sorry, Charlie," she finally said. "I know I told you I'd be ready, and I missed you so much—but I'm just not there yet."

She looked down, her eyes beginning to pool.

"I'm just so scared of getting pregnant and ending up like my parents. I don't want that life for us! I mean, I want kids some-day. But not now. We have so much still to do in school and—"

"It's not a problem, Little Darlin'," he said. Then he coughed and gave a little laugh. "Well, maybe it's a little prob-lem, but don't you fret any."

He took her in his arms and embraced her. She hugged him back with tears now running down her face.

"I'm not sayin' it's easy, because you know how much I love you and how wild you drive me. But we've got time, and I can wait."

Just a year later, Charlie found himself gazing into those big blue eyes, with Cassie melting into his sparkling emerald ones. And Cassie said what he had known she would someday say:

"I do" in front of so many family and friends gathered at his family's Texas ranch.

Mr. and Mrs. Tanum then rode off in a horse-drawn carriage, waving at the smiling faces throwing rice from the steps of the house.

As they rode away on that warm August day, Cassie turned to her husband and leaned in close with a twinkle in her eyes he hadn't seen before.

"Why, Mr. Tanum, I do believe it's much too warm for that jacket you're wearing."

She relieved him of it while she surrounded his mouth with tiny kisses. Then she loosened the bolo tie he always wore to get to the buttons on his shirt.

Charlie grinned at her and started to pull off the tie, but she gently moved his hand away and kissed it.

"Not the bolo," she whispered in his ear. "That will be the last to go once we get to the inn."

She adjusted the wedding veil blowing across her face, tucked it behind her, and kissed him again, this time on the throat, taking the tie in her teeth.

"Darlin'," she said, "do these horses go any faster? I'm ready to be in our bridal suite."

Charlie gave her a double take. "Really? Yee-haw! It's about time, Little Darlin'!"

He sang the rest of the way to the inn.

The first five years of marriage were blissful. Life was an exciting adventure as they completed school and worked to achieve their goals. They never stopped until they accomplished exactly what they wanted—whether it was a column in the newspaper or an article in a magazine for Cassie or great reviews on Charlie's latest novel.

They bought a condo in a high-rise building with city views and within walking distance to shops and restaurants. The university was also close enough so Charlie could still teach, which helped fatten the piggy bank. Life was good—great, actually.

Philly was the perfect city for them. There was never a dull moment in the lives of Charlie and Cassie Tanum. They both loved their careers. They always had good friends around, but the couple was also totally content to hide out in their abode for sometimes a whole weekend happily just loving each other.

One September evening, Cassie wandered up to Charlie and closed the laptop he was working on to get his attention. He laughed as she hugged his neck from behind.

"What would you say to having another Little Darlin' in your life?" she asked.

Charlie took her hands and kissed her fingers. "You're all the darlin' I need. As a matter of fact," he said, standing and tipping her chin to look into her eyes, "how about I have my Little Darlin' right now?"

He nibbled on her lips, then gave her that smile with those twinkling emerald eyes already undressing her.

Cassie smiled as happy tears began rolling down her cheeks. "Well, I'm not sure how to say this . . . You're going to be a daddy!"

"*What?*"

He let out a whoop as he picked her up and swung her around.

"I can't believe it!" he exclaimed, his words coming fast. "But how? I mean, we weren't even planning this. We knew we wanted this someday but—oh, whatever! Who cares about that? You're going to be a mom!"

He kissed her and wiped her tears. Once again speaking without words, they each confirmed that the time was now right.

"We're gonna be parents, Little Darlin'!"

Chapter 8

THE SECRET IS OUT

October 2004—Abemly Shores

STANDING AT HIS BEDROOM CLOSET, Jonas had just pulled his shirt over his head when JJ marched up with his arms across his chest.

"Daddy, are you and Cassie going out again tonight? I want to go too!" JJ insisted. "How am I gonna figure out if she'll be my new mom if I don't get to go on a date with you guys? Come on, Daddy! I'm six and a half now, you know!"

"Hey, bud," Jonas replied, a bit irked but chuckling all the same. "Cassie and I are just friends who like to do things together, you know!" he added, imitating his son. "We're going to a scary movie tonight anyway, and I know you wouldn't like it. Besides, I thought you were all excited to spend the night at Joey's house."

Joey was the nine-year-old son of Donny, Cassie's cousin. He was like a nephew to her.

"It'll be a real guys' night—pizza, popcorn, movies," Jonas said. "And the best will be going in the backyard when it gets dark to chase after fireflies and play hide-and-seek with the neighbor kids."

Not too sure he was convincing enough, Jonas continued, "I remember how cool it was when my best friend and I had overnights. Friday night couldn't come fast enough for me."

JJ dropped his hands to his side and looked at his feet while he dug a toe into the floor. "I thought Mommy was your best friend. Did you have overnights with her at Grandma and Grandpa Sills's cottage when you were six and a half?"

Trying to hold himself together, Jonas squatted down in front of JJ. He cupped his chin and lifted the boy's head to be eye to eye with him.

"Yes, of course Mommy was my best friend. I'm not trying to replace her in either of our lives—you know that, right?" Dabbing at a lone tear on JJ's cheek, he went on, "You and I will always love and remember Mommy. Heck, every time I look at you, I see her and think about how you are the best of her and me all mixed together!"

He took the small boy in his embrace.

"I love you so much, JJ. We are going to have such a good life, you and I." He loosened his hold and rested his hands on JJ's shoulders, giving him a big grin. "And hey, for your information, mister—Billy was my best friend when I was your age. Your mom and I were friends too, but we were older when we became really close. You'll understand that someday," he said with a wink.

Taking his dad by the hand, JJ looked up and said, "I love you. Now let's go, or you'll be late for your 'friend date'!"

After dropping JJ off at Joey's house, Jonas headed over to pick up Cassie. He opened the car door for her with a smile.

"So, are you ready for the scare of your life? I've been waiting for this movie to come out for the longest time! It's supposed to be a real vampire thriller."

Cassie's eyes darted down as she sat in the car with her legs still facing the open door. "I know how much you want to see it, but I was thinking more along the lines of getting a bite to eat and following it up with a walk. It's a pretty night. And, well, I have some things I need to share with you." She attempted a smile, but it was more of a frown. "I'm really sorry, but I have to get this off my chest, and tonight feels like the right time."

Jonas nodded and motioned for her to swing her legs into the car. He gave a little smile. "Sure, that's fine. I guess the vamps will have to do with two less buckets of blood tonight," he said with a laugh. "What type of food are you hungry for?"

"Hmm, after the vampire comment, I'd appreciate anything that isn't red. Yuck!" She rolled her eyes at him playfully. "Actually, breakfast food sounds good. How about the Waffle House?"

"Really? I can be up for that—something different, even though it can't touch Jonas's Fine Café," he said with a smirk and a wink.

The Waffle House was out of town, just off the highway. During the drive there, Cassie just looked out the window and said nothing. She seemed nervous and worried, not her usual bubbly, excited self.

The meal came and went—very uneventful and rather quiet except for casual aboveboard conversation. They left the diner and headed back to Abemly Shores, such a pretty place to walk along the boulevard with its flowering shrubs and old oak trees. He parked the car in front of Book Benders instead of the café to avoid being spotted and called in to work for some reason. It was a beautiful, clear, crisp October night with stars so bright they lit up the sky. It was so light, it seemed more like dusk than ten o'clock.

Cassie took his hand as they walked. They breathed in the cool night air and occasionally stopped to look at the stars.

"It's a beautiful night, isn't it, Jonas?" Tears began forming in her eyes.

When Jonas noticed the tears, he took a tissue from his pocket and wiped them away very gently. "What is it, Cassie? Is what you wanted to tell me that bad? Are you sick? Did something happen at work that got you all upset?"

"No, no. It's nothing like that. Come on—let's sit on that bench under those pines near the little pond."

With his hand still in hers, she guided him to the spot and pulled him gently down to the bench with her. But then she abruptly jumped up and began pacing.

"What the heck is going on with you, Cassie? You're beginning to frighten me! Please stop stalling and start talking before you have both of us in a panic. Otherwise, I think I'm gonna jump in the pond!"

That sounded so absurd that Cassie started laughing—a laugh that changed quickly to overwhelming bouts of gasping for air, then uncontrollable sobbing. Jonas grabbed her arms to try shaking her out of her hysterics.

"What is it? Tell me, and tell me now!"

She melted into his arms and continued to sob. He just stood there and held her tight, hoping to calm the fear or sadness that had engulfed her.

Taking several deep, cleansing breaths, Cassie sat down next to her friend. She took his hands in hers and looked him straight in the eye.

"You know I was married years ago when I lived in Philly. Charlie was a very charismatic man. He drove me crazy at first, never leaving me alone when he was a teaching assistant in my first college class." She chuckled under her breath as she pictured him in her mind. "He just knew what he wanted and wouldn't take no for an answer, no matter how long it took me to accept him into my heart."

"Yes, I know that," Jonas said, practically interrupting her as his impatience grew. "You also told me Charlie took some secretive writing assignment and never returned. So what's gotten into you? Have you gotten word that Charlie's body was found?"

"No, I don't have any news about Charlie. It's nothing like that." She let go of his hands to take a tissue from her purse and blow her nose. "Oh, Jonas, there's so much more to the story than what I've told you."

Jonas was perplexed and frustrated. "I don't understand. What more could there be? I thought we were good friends and shared everything. I've told you all about Charlotte and my in-laws—you've even been to their home several times. What haven't you told me?"

"Jonas! Would you please stop interrogating me and just listen?" She sighed. "I'm sorry, but this is hard to talk about. But you're right: we are good friends, and we should share everything. Our friendship means the world to me, so I can't let it go any further unless you know everything."

She took another breath, then slowly blew it out as she organized her thoughts.

"The last few months Charlie and I had together were amazing. We loved our careers. We had a great group of supportive friends and family. Then the most wonderful thing happened—I found out I was pregnant. When I told Charlie, he just about went ballistic with joy!"

Jonas opened his mouth, but she covered it with her hand.

"Hush. Don't you understand how hard it is to finally tell you this—how hard it is for my ears to hear it? Please, Jonas."

Jonas wove his fingers through his black hair and massaged his head. As anxious as he was, he decided to let Cassie take the time she needed to tell her tale. She sniffled and took another deep breath before continuing.

Cassie had been a city girl until she met Charlie. But the couple enjoyed visiting his parents' T and R Ranch in Texas as often as they could. Cassie learned to ride horses and absolutely fell in love with the sweetest, gentlest horse they had. Charlie told her Selly was a great old gal and could always be trusted with her rider.

Cassie and Charlie visited the ranch when she was a little over five months pregnant. They framed an ultrasound picture in pink to reveal the sex of the baby to the future grandparents. Charlie's parents were so excited, they just couldn't wait to hang

JUST SOMETHING IN THE WIND

the picture on the family wall. Charlie and Cassie had a giggle when his parents hung it right in the middle of all the ancestors.

That night at the ranch was so perfect. Cassie and Charlie sat together on that big porch swing, listening to the crickets as the warm breeze tickled their noses. They laughed because try as they might, there was no counting the stars. They picked out the brightest star and talked about how they would tell their daughter it was her special star. They shared their hopes and dreams for their wonderful little girl. After making love that night, they just held each other and fell asleep with their hands clasped over Cassie's belly—protecting and loving the new life living inside.

The morning breeze came through the bedroom windows, bringing the fragrant smell of dew on a freshly mowed lawn. Charlie turned on his side to look at Cassie and say he loved her.

Cassie would never hear him speak those words so sincerely again.

Charlie claimed it was a perfect day to ride. Cassie was nervous about riding, though. The last time she rode, she was only three months along. Now she was bigger and showing much more. She was also concerned that her balance was becoming a bit awkward.

Charlie's mother agreed with Cassie, saying it wasn't a good idea for her to ride. But Charlie was adamant it was safe.

"Little Darlin', you're safer on old Selly than you are walking to the corral!" he insisted.

Cassie didn't want to disappoint him. When she agreed to go, Charlie picked her up and swung her around—as best he could. They walked hand in hand to the barn and saddled up.

When he helped Cassie up onto Selly, he whispered to the old girl to take extra special care of both of his darlin's.

Cassie had to agree—it was such a beautiful day for a ride. They headed out in a familiar direction and took it very leisurely. After about an hour of riding, they headed back, talking once again about their expanding family and how they'd get their little girl a pony of her own someday.

But suddenly, Selly started snorting, then bowing her head sharply, thrashing and pawing the ground. Cassie tried to hang on as best she could, but it was like riding a bronco—not that she had ever tried that. Cassie did her best to calm Selly down and divert her in the other direction.

But then Cassie heard it—that horrible rattling sound. There it was in all its hateful glory, with that unmistakable diamond design trailing down its scaly back. It was prepared to strike. Poor frightened Selly thrashed more and more.

"Just hold on!" Charlie yelled. He was struggling with his own horse, trying desperately to turn the frightened animal around so he could reach Cassie and Selly.

His words had barely left his mouth when Selly reared once again. Cassie went down, rolling and flipping until finally landing on her side in a crumpled ball.

Selly raced off, and so did Charlie's horse once he dismounted and rushed to Cassie's side. Charlie had to carry his wife back to the ranch, cradling her, trying to protect her and the baby.

"Hold on, my Little Darlin's," he said through his sobs. "It'll be okay. Just hold on."

But Cassie realized she was losing their little girl—she was dying at that very moment. So much pain. So much blood.

Cassie went unconscious.

The next thing Cassie knew, she was waking up in bed—the bed where, only hours before, the little family of three had slept together with happy dreams of their future. When she tried to open her bruised and swollen eyes, she saw Charlie and his parents crying. A doctor was there as well. He just frowned and shook his head.

Once Cassie stabilized, an ambulance transported her to the nearest hospital, where she spent the first weeks of recovery. Eventually she went home, nursing a broken arm and bruised ribs.

Their lives were never the same. Charlie blamed himself for insisting Cassie go riding, despite her and his mother's worries. He began hiding from anything and anyone that meant anything to him. He closed himself off from Cassie. No matter how hard she tried to convince him it was no one's fault, he just wouldn't listen. He was a totally different person from that fun-loving, charismatic Texan she had fallen in love with and married. That man seemed to have died along with their baby girl. Nothing mattered anymore. Charlie let his work slip to the point where he was laid off. They encouraged him to rest and return when he felt able.

Then one day, Charlie told Cassie he had received a long-term freelance writing assignment in a classified location. He couldn't tell her where he was going, only that he felt it would be good to go away for a while. He said he still loved her, then packed up and left.

Cassie heard from him a few times during the first weeks, then the calls were far between as the months went by. She heard nothing for so long, until one day two officers came to the house. They said Charlie was missing and presumed dead.

Cassie decided to leave it all behind. She left Philly and moved to Abemly Shores, where her cousin Donny lived.

Too spent to cry anymore, Cassie rested her head on Jonas's shoulder and looked up to the clear sky, searching for the star of her unborn child. She hugged her stomach, then leaned over and began sobbing and retching. She quickly turned away and vomited. Reliving those horrific experiences made her physically and mentally sick.

Jonas was in tears as he reached for her. "Oh God, Cassie. I can't believe what you went through. I'm so sorry. I just can't imagine your pain."

She wiped her face with a tissue, then took a long breath. "I'm sorry I kept this from you. But I've tried so hard to erase it all from my mind these past few years. I couldn't imagine burdening anyone else with it."

Jonas touched his forehead to hers. "Don't you know you can always lean on your best friend?"

Cassie nodded and smiled. "I know. I really do. But it's just so hard . . ."

Jonas held her hand as she let out great sobs of both sadness and relief.

A sudden flash of lightning and an angry wind blew dozens of pine cones off the trees, swirling them around before crashing, broken, to the ground. The wind seemed to be crying with Cassie.

Chapter 9

A HAPPENSTANCE MEETING

February 2006—Outside Abemly Shores

It was a gloomy morning, and Savannah Sheridan was on her way to visit her family after several weeks of exhilarating yet exhausting concerts.

Not a fan of interstates, she was on some backroad in South Carolina, not far from the ocean. Every now and then, she'd put her window down a bit to smell the fresh breeze. As Savannah drove along, gazing at the picturesque surroundings, she gave her long auburn curls a toss. She thought of how wonderful it would be to wake with this same sun streaming through her window and to take in the fresh scent of the ocean and the serene landscape. She turned on the radio and swayed with the music while catching a glimpse of the rolling ocean waves in the distance, orchestrating a composition of its own.

Born in Georgia, Savannah and her sister, Adrianna, grew up in a home where music was abundant. Their parents, Dorothy and Harold Sheridan, were partners in a law firm, but they always joked that they had been musicians in a former life. Loving music and theater as they did, Dotty and Hal guided their daughters into the world of the arts from a very young age. During the elementary and high school years, piano lessons were always a given. Being a very close family, they enjoyed musical activities together. Theater performances and concerts of all types were a constant among the Sheridan family weekend outings.

The girls both attended college. While Savannah continued with her love of music, Adrianna found that her greater love was a medical student named Simon.

After receiving her master's degree in music, Savannah began touring the United States, performing her original jazz pieces. She built quite a following. Extremely successful and blessed with talent, Savannah soon established herself as an accomplished pianist and composer. She was well known across the country for her bluesy, mesmerizing sound.

Touring was exciting and enriching, but Savannah had now been on the road for two years. Floating from music halls to theaters left her very little time for family. She decided to find a permanent residence.

Savannah had just finished a phenomenal performance at Carnegie Hall—the second time she had performed there in two years. She was elated that she had been asked to come back. Mac McCallum, her boyfriend, was in the audience, sitting in pretty much the same spot he sat in at every theater so she could always pick him out. Dotty and Hal had hoped to attend, but Adrianna was expecting her second child any day and needed to have Grandma and Grandpa close by for babysitting.

Savannah had planned on driving to Georgia the morning after the concert. She was looking forward to visiting family and hopefully meeting the newest addition. She had wanted Mac to drive with her, but as always, his business plans got in the way. He had made it just in the nick of time for the concert, and he already had another meeting scheduled in DC for the next day.

This, of course, meant he couldn't drive with Savannah to see her family. It was too far to drive nonstop without Mac's copiloting, so she drove as far as she could, then stopped at a motel for the night.

She hated staying in those roadside motels alone. As much as she loved meeting fans, being recognized at motels could sometimes be awkward. Some people just stared at her or whispered behind her back. And more importantly, Savannah found it creepy to pull in to a motel without even knowing whether the area was safe or seedy.

Savannah was exhausted from the concert and the argument with Mac. She quickly made her way to her room and fell asleep the moment she turned off the lights. She woke early the next morning, snagged a coffee, and started the last leg of her drive home to see her family.

Winding along the coastal roads, she couldn't help but reflect upon her relationship with Mac. What happened? How did it get to this point?

Mac interfering with Savannah's best-laid plans was nothing new, but it was getting more and more on her nerves. She was beginning to wonder if she had fallen off the top of Mac's priority list. He always promised that nothing was more important than their relationship, that he'd never be one of those guys who let work come between them, that he'd always be there for her. Ha!

This time, she'd had enough of his nonsense. There in the hotel after the concert, she came right out and accused him of not caring and not trying to keep the relationship alive. She even suggested that perhaps he was seeing another woman and that was why he kept disappearing—after all, it had happened before!

In college, they had been so close, doing everything together. Even after college, when she began touring, Mac had been so supportive of her music. He followed her to as many concerts as he was able.

But then he took the big promotion, and things changed. A corner office and traveling all over the world meeting new people. There was that "slipup" (as he called it) in Paris with a business associate—blond, long legs, gorgeous, and a French accent to boot. It wasn't his fault. "She fed me wine and took advantage of my loneliness," he said.

At the time, Savannah forgave him, remembering the sweet innocence of their first time. He was her first and only. Now, however, she had a different view of the "slipup."

I can't believe I forgave him for that! Savannah thought to herself.

"Sometimes Mac makes me so angry!" she growled out loud.

Deciding to put Mac out of her mind, she began singing with the radio as she continued her drive along the coast.

Suddenly, from out of nowhere, a ferocious gust of wind kicked up. It ripped a huge, mangled tree branch from its trunk and threw it a few yards in front of the car. There was no way to swerve or slow down. Savannah heard the crunching of metal. She lost control. The car hurtled toward a bank of trees at a speed of forty-five miles per hour.

Then just as suddenly, the car slowed down as if it had a mind of its own. Savannah watched as the steering wheel seemed to take over, gently bringing her to a smooth stop on the side of the road.

White knuckled and in disbelief, she glanced out the side mirror. *What in the world just happened?* she thought. *That wind came from out of the blue. It was like a twenty-second tornado—so absurd!*

With another glance in the side mirror, she could see the branch had caused her to blow a tire. Who knew what other damage there had been. But it could have been much worse, had it not been for that eerie rescue with the car all but driving itself.

With her initial shock slowly wearing off, Savannah put the car in park. She turned off the ignition with a very shaky hand, unbuckled and flipped her seat belt away, then leaned back in her seat, took a deep breath, and began weeping.

What am I doing with my life, driving up and down the coast performing for people I don't even know? I should be with people I love and care about. This is a ridiculous way to live! I'm pushing twenty-nine. At the very least, I should have a specific place to call home.

She stared at herself in the rearview mirror and saw the same hazel eyes as her father's. Instantly, she couldn't help but think of his words of wisdom: "Just be who you are, and treat everyone with kindness and respect—always. Then good things will come your way." A small smile lit up those eyes that were cloned from Harold Sheridan.

Finally pulling herself together, Savannah used the GPS on her cell phone to find out where she was and to give a heads-up to Hal and Dotty that she'd be late getting home. She found the name of a café in a nearby town and got a quick glimpse of the directions right before her phone went dead.

"Not now—no! No!" she shouted.

With dread, she realized she had been so mad after her argument with Mac that she had forgotten to charge her phone as usual. Once again, it was all Mac's fault.

"Why is this happening to me?" she screamed angrily.

She reached in the back seat for her purse and the old coat and gloves she kept in the car for emergencies. She took her phone charger too, just in case she ever found electricity in this godforsaken place. If she had read the directions right, the café was just over the next hill, around the bend, and only a mile and a half up the road. *Only.*

With a huff, she wrote a note with her emergency information and shoved it behind the wiper blade. *Knowing my luck, it'll start raining, and no one will be able to read it*, she thought. She set the hazard lights and locked the door.

Savannah took another look around, then took yet another deep breath.

Enough whining, she told herself. *Let's get to it!*

With that, she was finished with negativity. She knew she should be glad she came through that ordeal as well as she did. Hanging her purse over her shoulder, she began the "short" hike toward town and Jonas's Fine Café. Along the way, she hoped she'd also find a "fine" service station to cure what ailed the car.

Chin up, she thought as she added a few skips in her step. *I should look at this as a new adventure. Who knows? This may be the beginning of something new in my life.* That made her grin.

As she walked, she thought more about her life. It truly was time to settle down and have a home—even if only to create a breathable space for when she needed a break.

But is Mac ready to settle down, though? she wondered. *And how am I supposed to know if he's the one to settle down with?*

The more she walked and thought, the more Mac's words and actions made sense. He wasn't ready at all. And quite frankly, he didn't seem to be the one. They were moving in opposite directions. She was finally seeing the light.

Maybe it's time for us to take a break, she concluded.

Upping her pace and snuggling into her coat, she began humming one of her more well-known compositions. Just as she was passing by some bushes near the road, she almost fell as she tripped over something. Thinking it was debris, she swung her foot back to kick it out of the way.

"Hey! That's not very nice!" came a voice from out of nowhere.

With a little shriek, Savannah stopped and set her foot abruptly on the ground. She turned to see where the voice had come from. To her surprise, two dark eyes peered out at her from behind the bushes. They belonged to a thin, dark-haired boy about eight years old who had stuck his leg out to get her attention. He was wearing a lightweight jacket that seemed to have a life of its own. The jacket was somehow wiggling and whining, but the boy held tight to whatever it was, holding his secret close.

"What have you got there, and why are you way out here by yourself?" Savannah asked gently, kneeling down to match the boy's height.

"First of all, I'm not alone," he said.

He opened his coat just enough for a small black nose to peek out. Next came a face with curly, dirty, no-longer-white fur. One ear was up, and the other flopped over.

"Second of all, I don't talk to strangers . . . usually. But I'm the one who started talking to you, so I guess I'm actually the stranger. I'm not a bad stranger, though. So it's okay—you can talk to me."

It was all she could do to keep from laughing. She didn't know whether to hug or scold him for being out on the road alone in the cold, dingy air.

"Hey, what were you humming before I almost made you fall?" the boy continued. The jiggling, wiggling jacket became more animated as he began talking faster and faster. "I think I've heard that music at my grandma's house. My grandma and grandpa like to play music together. How do you know that one? Do you play music too? I can play the piano," he said. He stood straighter than before, attempting to look at least an inch taller while proudly proclaiming his talent.

"Actually, I wrote that music that you say your grandparents play. I'm what's called a composer. And I love to play piano, just like you. I'm so happy to hear that all of you enjoy my music."

He stood there looking at her with those big black eyes. He searched her face as he listened to her story.

"My name is Savannah. I was on my way to visit my family in Georgia, but I have a flat tire, so I'm walking to town to see about getting it fixed. I saw there's a place called Jonas's Fine Café. Have you heard of—"

Before she could finish, the boy cried out, "No! You can't go there! He's a mean man! He doesn't want to help anyone, he hates dogs, and I hate him!"

"Whoa!" Savannah took his shoulders to calm him down. "Wait a minute—is Jonas the reason you ran away with the dog? What did he do? He didn't hurt you, did he?"

He pulled away from her and let out a sob. "I don't have to tell you anything 'cuz you're a stranger, and I don't talk to strangers!"

The boy began to gasp loudly from his hysterics and the cold wind suddenly kicking up from the ocean. Savannah placed her hands on his shoulders again.

"Hold on there, buddy. I just told you my name and my story. And remember, you're the stranger, right? You're the one who stopped me. I still don't even know your name."

The boy nodded, calming a little. He moved in closer to her for warmth and comfort. She held him with the wiggly, jiggling jacket between them.

"I'm Jessup Jonas Beckman," he said, trying to take breaths in between speaking, "but they call me JJ."

Savannah looked at him in surprise. "Jessup Jonas? As in Jonas's Fine Café? Is Jonas your dad?" The puzzle pieces were starting to come together.

JJ nodded.

"Well, JJ, why don't you walk along with me into town? You can introduce me to your wiggly friend and explain why you two would rather be out in the cold ocean air than home having breakfast in a nice, warm kitchen."

As they walked, JJ told Savannah about the puppy he found while taking the shortcut home from school. Concerned that it was lost and that the owner would be worried about it, he went to several homes on the edge of town, asking if they knew to whom it belonged. He came to a little house with

GAIL WALLACH BUELL
GAIL WALLACH BUELL

pretty lace curtains and an old-fashioned mailbox with a pretty picture on it.

"The man that answered the door was really nice," JJ told Savannah. "He told me to check with the lady who owns the bookstore." Giving the puppy a kiss on the head and tucking it back in his jacket, he continued. "My pup—I mean, *the* pup—started yipping like she was really excited when we walked up the steps to the bookstore and pulled on the bell. I recognized the nice lady when she came to the door. She's friends with my grandma and grandpa. She told me I didn't need to ring the bell because it's a store. But I just stood there outside the door 'cuz I didn't think I could bring a dog into a store. So I showed her the pup, and the lady got tears in her eyes."

JJ wiped his own damp eyes as he went on with his story. "She said this little female was the only one left in the litter Josie, her dog, had just had. She said Josie and the pup somehow got out of the house the day before. She was sad and scared about them being lost but didn't know where to look."

He hugged the puppy closer to him.

"She told me Josie came home late that night, and it looked like she had a run-in with another animal. The lady was worried the other animal had gotten the pup. The woman was so happy to see the pup safe, she asked me to please keep her. So I promised to love her and take care of her always. And I *always* keep my promises."

Tears began to well up in his eyes again.

"But then when I took the pup home, my dad told me I'd have to give her back to the lady. But I didn't want to give her back. I promised to take care of her, and I always keep my promises!" he said again, this time through sniffles. "Dad said

74
74

we can't have a dog in our place 'cuz we live over the diner. I told him I'd take good care of her and feed her and walk her! But he said she'd need room to run. Well, yeah, I guess we don't really have a yard."

He looked up at Savannah as he hugged the pup in his jacket.

"I get what he was saying. But I really wanted this pup, so I yelled that I was taking my pup and going where no one could find us. And I ran away!" He lifted his chin defiantly, then softened. "But really, my dad isn't a bad man. I miss him already."

Savannah listened with a face full of concern. She decided to redirect the boy into something more positive.

"So, JJ, you haven't officially introduced me to your wiggly little friend, and I'd hate to remain strangers," Savannah said with a coy grin. "Do you have a name for her yet?"

He opened his jacket again just enough for the pup to show its dirty, curly head and one paw. "Savannah, this is Jacey. She's a mixed-up poodle."

Savannah laughed. "I think what you mean is a poodle mix." She carefully took the pup's paw in her gloved hand. "It's very nice to meet you, little Jacey." She looked back at JJ. "What a wonderful name you gave her!"

"I know it's a wonderful name because my mom named her. Uh, I mean . . ." he stammered and sniffled. "I mean, that's the name she would have named a pup if she was still here, instead of heaven."

Now tears welled up in Savannah's eyes. She zipped up JJ's jacket and put her arm around his shoulder. Together they walked into town and straight to Jonas's Fine Café—where she was ready to have a heart-to-heart with Mr. Jonas himself.

Chapter 10

EXPLORING ABEMLY

February 2006—Abemly Shores

FINALLY REACHING JONAS'S FINE CAFÉ, Savannah came to a halt on the brick sidewalk right in front. She bent at the waist with hands on her hips, trying to catch her breath from the run-walk following JJ to town. The chilly, brisk air felt cold as it filled her lungs. She stood up and stretched her back.

"That's it! I have to start exercising more." She looked at JJ's grin and added, "And maybe I also need to take up running."

JJ reached for her hand, wanting some backup for himself and his wiggling jacket before they went up against the "mean" Jonas.

Savannah took his hand, then took a step toward the café. She froze. *What a lovely, welcoming place!* It felt as though she had been there before—maybe just in her dreams. At the very least, she felt an odd connection to the town. She shivered as an unfamiliar tingle shot through her when she and JJ walked through the door.

The café had the look and feel of an Irish pub, allowing a casual, cozy atmosphere. The floor was a dark, warm knotty pine that had seemingly been there forever. The walls were dark yet colorful because they were peppered with hundreds of hand-written notes and pictures, apparently given to the owners of the café. Several booths surrounded the walls, while round tables filled the center of the room. Lovely cushions and pillows covered in deep-colored plaid fabric added to the pub atmosphere. In one corner, Savannah spotted a small dance floor. She smiled. Upbeat music was playing in the background, and a chalkboard over the bar featured a handwritten menu. The smell of barbecue and wood smoke was inviting and oh-so comforting!

Savannah felt the wiggly jacket at her back and realized JJ was hiding from something or someone. She twisted around to smile at him, but he wasn't smiling at all.

When Savannah turned back, she was confronted with the most amazing dark, almost black eyes she'd ever seen. The eyes were angry as they looked out at her. The hair under his backward-facing ball cap was black as coal, just grazing his shirt collar. It framed the strong, fine, chiseled face.

"What are you doing with my son?" he barked. "Where has he been? Why do you have him? And, well, who in the heck are you?"

The man then reached behind her, grabbed the boy's arm, and brought him into the light, wiggly jacket and all. JJ was obviously frightened and trying not to cry.

"JJ, I was so worried about you—so scared. I didn't have any idea where to look. Thank God you're okay. I would be lost without you! Don't you know you're my whole world? I love you so much!" He took the little boy into his arms, giving him a bear hug and a kiss on the head.

JJ looked up at his dad's slim six-two stature with tears in his eyes. "I'm sorry I ran away from you. I was mad. You didn't want me to have Jacey."

The pup peeked out with her tongue lapping. JJ took her out of the jacket for Jonas to see. Jonas gave her a light pat on the head and gave his son a loving smile.

"Um, Dad, this is my friend Savannah. I found her stuck on the road when the storm came up and wrecked her car—"

"Hey, wait just one minute, bud! What storm? It's been sunny all morning, even if a little chilly." He frowned a bit. "I've told you time and again that it's not right to tell a lie."

"I am *not* lying—just ask Savannah. She hit a big branch when the wind suddenly came up, and then it blew over to the side of the road!"

Looking from his son to Savannah, Jonas apologized. "Sorry about this. Ever since we lost Charlotte, JJ's mom, he tends to exaggerate a bit."

He went to shake Savannah's hand, but she held her hand up in the air as if to stop him.

"Actually, in JJ's defense, that's pretty much how it happened. Winds really did come out of nowhere. I thought it was a tornado! It came and went in a matter of seconds—strangest thing I've ever experienced. I'll tell you the whole story if you can take a break."

Jonas softened. "I'm sorry about all this. I'm sorry I yelled at you. I was just so scared about almost losing my son. I can't tell you how much it means to me that you brought him back safely. Thank you so much."

He tentatively reached out once again to shake her hand. Electricity seemed to shoot between them when they touched. For a moment, he was mystified as he looked into her hazel eyes. She was just as hypnotized by his. He dropped her hand to break the connection.

"How can I ever repay you? Wait—you both must be starved. Eggs and pancakes along with one coffee, one hot chocolate with whipped cream, and one bowl of water comin' up." Before he went off to the kitchen, he ruffled JJ's hair and gave Jacey another pat on the head. "Son, you'd better take the pup upstairs for now. You know animals are not allowed in the restaurant."

As JJ rushed upstairs, Jonas turned to Savannah once again.

"I'm sorry about taking this out on you. You gotta understand that it's just been him and me for the past five years—since we lost his mom. Thanks so much for bringing my boy home."

He smiled shyly, showing a dimple just above the point where his mouth curved into a contagious grin. He casually touched her shoulder and nodded to a table near the small stage area.

"Why don't you have a seat and get comfortable? JJ and I will join you after I whip up some omelets for us all." He tossed her that shy smile as he walked away.

Over a pleasant breakfast, Jonas agreed to let Jacey take up permanent residence in JJ's room—under the condition that JJ was to be in charge of her and take care of all her needs. Savannah had her say, confirming just how much the boy cared for the dog.

"Well, I suppose I better go check in with the service station," Savannah said as they finished their meal. "I'll need them to go tow the car and fix the tire."

Jonas stood up as Savannah rose to her feet. "Again, I can't apologize enough, nor can I thank you enough. Please stop in at the café whenever you're in the area."

Savannah was already out on the street when JJ ran after her and gave her such a big hug that he almost knocked her over once again. She touched her lips to the top of his head and whispered, "I'm sure your mom is so proud of you. I know she's always watching over you and your dad."

JJ grinned sheepishly. "Yes, she is, and she's looking out for you too. See ya!"

Very confused and a little stunned at his words, she shooed him along. "Now run along home before your dad thinks you ran away again!"

She watched him skip, hop, and jump happily back toward the diner. A warmth radiated through her as well as an emptiness. Tears ran down her cheeks. She smiled to herself.

Boy, it must be something about this town that has me draining my tear ducts.

The service station quickly dispatched their tow truck and promised they'd get right to work fixing her vehicle. Savannah decided to bundle up and use the time to walk down Main Street. She quickly fell in love with the sweet little town.

The streetlights were actually gas lanterns. They flickered even during the daylight hours. Wooden benches graced the paved sidewalks and were adorned with arrays of flowers and shrubs. Even the boulevard boasted an occasional streetlight, and mature live oak trees with mystical moss draped over their crooked branches. The trees bowed as if to shield the townsfolk from harm. Savannah could feel the town's rich history.

While meandering, Savannah found a coffee shop housed in a quaint little bookshop. The name on the shingle read "Book Benders—Mona Argyle, Proprietor." Savannah assumed this was the bookshop JJ had mentioned as he described his adventures with Jacey.

She opened the door, causing the old-fashioned bell to ring and alert the proprietor. Taking off her gloves and rubbing her hands together, she announced a cheery "Hello! Anyone here?"

A familiar song in a pleasant voice came through from somewhere in the back of the shop. "I'm here! I'll be with you in a moment. Just adding wood to the fire—it's so cold out."

A little jovial woman came out from the back room, moving rather gingerly with her hand on her back. "Hello, I'm Mona Argyle. I apologize for taking so long. I just don't get around as well as I used to."

Just then, a curly white poodle with apricot markings sauntered in and sat right down next to Mona, looking up at her for the next order to be given.

"Oh, and this is my special girl, my Josie. I don't know how I'd get by without her."

"Hello, I'm Savannah Sheridan, and I'm very glad to meet you both." She first took the woman's hand, then bent down when the dog delicately offered her paw. "I believe I've already met your pretty little pup, Jacey," Savannah said as she took the paw in her hand.

Mona nodded and smiled knowingly. "Ah, so you've met JJ. Here, come tell me all about it. I can use a little break, anyway."

Mona fixed up a tray with coffee and scones and brought it to the cozy sitting area amongst stacks of older and historical books. She sat down with Josie by her side and motioned for Savannah to make herself comfortable too. They took advantage of the warmth from the fireplace as Savannah shared the recent adventure that brought her to Abemly Shores and how she'd met Jonas and JJ.

"I'm so intrigued by this lovely little town," she said. "Its history. Its people in the present as well as in the past."

Mona reached over and took a book off a shelf. She peeked over her reading glasses at her guest as she smiled coyly and blew at least some of the dust off the well-aged book.

"Good enough!"

She opened it and pointed out some of the unique aspects and history of the little town Savannah found herself falling in love with. As they pored over the book, the women had so much to share and had formed such camaraderie that they lost track of time.

"Oh my gosh, Mona—I can't believe how long we've been talking!" Savannah exclaimed with a laugh as she checked her watch. She smiled warmly and clasped Mona's hand. "I feel like I have a new best friend. But I'd better get going. It's so nice of you to share your love and knowledge of Abemly Shores with me."

"Savannah, wait—one more thing." Mona stood and handed her the old book with the dusty leather cover. "I would love for you to have this book—you don't owe me anything for it. All I ask is that you read it through when you have the opportunity, enjoy it, and then come back for coffee sometime so you can share what you've learned and ask any questions you might have."

With Josie on her heels, Mona walked Savannah to the porch and grasped her hands once again. "I just have a feeling that Abemly Shores will be seeing more of you in the future," she said with a wink.

Fortunately, a tire change was all her car had needed. There wasn't any other damage to keep her from driving home. Soon, she was on her way.

Thinking of the people she had met and how the town was drawing her in, Savannah decided to take a bit of a detour and check out the surrounding area. The gloom of the morning had given way to the warmth and glow of the sun. Even though it was still cool, the briskness and smell of the sea air hauntingly called to her.

Just like a picture postcard, she thought as she spotted an intriguing winding gravel road lined with trees. A No Trespassing sign hung helter-skelter on a post. Not taking the warning too seriously, Savannah parked on the side of the road and began walking.

It smells like a mix of sea air and sweet flowers—it's amazing how beautiful the day has become, she thought.

The celestial queue of oak trees created a comforting feeling of protection as her heart led her farther up the road. Before following the bend, she detected a heady scent of wood burning, and then through the trees she heard music. All-too-familiar music. It was the sound of piano keys and the mellow eloquence of a French horn smoothly pouring out the sultry rhythm she knew so well. It was *her* music. Someone was playing Savannah's own composition with such deep feeling in this magical place.

A few steps farther, she saw it and gasped—the blue two-story cottage with its pristine white trim and wide expanse of covered porch facing the ocean. She felt it again, only much stronger. That feeling of being called to a place, a place you have never been to before but overwhelmingly calls you as if welcoming you home.

Chapter 11

MUSICAL ACQUAINTANCES

February 2006—Abemly Shores

SAVANNAH PLACED HER HAND ON HER HEART—it was beating so fast! She told herself to relax.

It's just a coincidence that this cottage is familiar. And the music? Well, people all over the United States listen to or play my music. Right?

Not quite succeeding at calming herself down, Savannah decided to walk to the door and introduce herself. She just had to—she was so curious. After all, the homeowners apparently appreciated jazz, and they sounded like accomplished musicians.

Taking a deep breath and attempting to smooth her hair to look presentable, she walked past the pretty flowerbeds leading to the front porch. There was a lovely set of wicker furniture with navy blue seats and red throw pillows, a chaise lounge, and two cozy rocking chairs. A telescope faced the water.

In addition, Savannah saw a beautiful double-wedding-ring quilt tossed haphazardly over the chaise. The quilt was in soft pastel colors and obviously well loved, judging by its tattered ends. As she looked closer, she saw small print in the corner of the quilt that read, "Made with love, Cecilia 1996." Something made her feel so sad about the inscription, but what, she wasn't sure. It was like an aura that stabs at your heart, leaving behind depression and sadness without rhyme or reason.

Suddenly, the music stopped. A tall, handsome gentleman with thick hair the same gray as his eyes opened the door. He frowned.

"Are you looking for someone in particular, or can you not read signs? This is private property, and you are trespassing!"

Just then, a pleasant woman with elegant stature and blond hair done up in a dancer's bun came to the door. She looked to be in her late fifties.

"Jonathon Jessup Sills, be nice! Why are you raising your voice?" She froze when she saw Savannah's face. "Oh my! Is this really who I think it is?"

With that, the man did a double take himself. "Wait—isn't this that composer?"

Without hesitation, Savannah spoke up. "Yes, it is," she teased. "I'm 'that composer,' Savannah Sheridan. I'm pleased to meet you."

She nervously touched her hand to her auburn hair and tucked it behind her ear. She smiled through curved, full lips and showed perfect teeth.

"So sorry to disturb you. It's just that I was drawn here somehow to this beautiful spot. And when I heard you playing my music, I couldn't help but introduce myself. I presume it was the two of you playing so beautifully?"

"Yes, it was!" The woman held her hand out to shake. "I'm Cecilia, and this is John. Please, won't you come in out of the chilly air? We're sorry for the lack of hospitality," she said in an apologetic voice and with a quick glance at her husband. "It's just that we don't get many random visitors out here. We're off the beaten path and a distance from town."

"I'd love to come in, if it's not too much trouble. Thank you!"

As she stepped over the threshold, Savannah knew she was home. What an odd feeling—being in a house you had never seen, with people who are total strangers, yet to have it all so comfortable and familiar.

The living room was charming with so many windows to let the light in and a welcoming stone fireplace from floor to ceiling. The best and most captivating sight, though, was what she saw between the corner windows. An antique grand piano shone like a priceless gem with the sun streaming across its gracious form.

John noticed her gaze. "Please—would you play for us?"

"I would be delighted. And please feel free to join in," she said, nodding to the French horn.

As Savannah's fingers moved expertly across the keys, she watched the rolling waves of the ocean through the expanse of windows. John picked up the French horn and began creating that pure tone that comes from that instrument alone. Smiling, Savannah took a deep breath. She hummed along with the magic created by her dancing fingers.

When they had finished, Cecilia applauded. "That was wonderful!" she exclaimed. "Let's celebrate with some coffee and sweets, shall we? Come—let's head into the kitchen."

As Savannah rose from the piano, John took her hand in his. "Thank you for sharing your gift with us and allowing us the pleasure of hearing you play your beautiful music." He seemed to be tearing up as he held her hand.

Savannah gave his hand a squeeze and returned his warm smile.

As Savannah passed through to the kitchen, she was drawn to a photo perched on a shelf of a handsome young couple holding a toddler with black hair and very large dark eyes.

"The man in that picture is familiar," she murmured out loud. "I think I know him . . ."

Suddenly, sadness rushed over her with such force she thought she might collapse. She quickly reached out for the closest chair, fell into it, and blacked out.

The next thing Savannah knew, she was opening her eyes and seeing the kind and concerned Cecilia sitting by her side, dabbing her forehead with a damp towel.

"How are you feeling now? You fainted, dear. Do you have any idea why?"

John came in and handed her a glass of water. "Would you like us to call a doctor?"

"Thank you, John, but I think I'll be fine," Savannah said, sitting up slowly. "Cecilia, is the invitation for coffee and sweets still open? Something sweet should help me get my energy back." She smiled graciously.

"Of course. Just take your time getting up. Here, let us help you to the kitchen table." John helped her up and followed her into the kitchen.

Once again, the picture caught her eye and shot over-whelming sadness to her heart. Her face went pale. John grabbed her, thinking she was going down again.

"What's wrong?" He then saw what she was staring at. "Is it the picture that upset you?" He looked at the picture too, let out a sad sigh, then looked back at Savannah with confusion. "But how in the world could it affect you so strongly like this?"

Savannah just shook her head and shrugged.

The three of them continued into the kitchen, which warmed Savannah immediately. The room was not large or extravagant. However, it was very cozy and welcoming, painted a creamy white with cabinets the same color and trimmed in the same blue as the outside shutters. The window over the sink looked out to the tree-lined path that had guided her to the house.

The other window, near the table, was large and had a window seat with a blue, cream, and rose floral cushion adorning it. A log cabin quilt of similar colors was folded neatly on it. It was the perfect stage setting for a lazy afternoon with a good book. A person could have sat right there all day watching the waves lapping the shore.

In the adjacent corner of the room was a lovely open fire-place complete with a cast-iron crane and a pot hanging on it. On one end of the mantel sat a fragrant candle and a few knick-knacks the Sillses had collected on various trips.

On the other end of the mantel appeared to be a family picture. It was John and Cecilia at a much younger age and a small blond-haired girl attempting an arabesque on the front porch. Next to it was a picture of that same small dark-haired boy standing on the front porch, blowing a random kiss for whomever to catch it.

Hanging above the mantel was a beautiful wreath of vines and dried flowers. Angled across the center of the wreath was a simple piece of driftwood with the initials C, J, and C, obviously carved by a child.

The trio enjoyed conversation with their coffee and scones while sitting at the round cherry kitchen table. The fire crackled in the background. Savannah was feeling much better, but the questions about that mysterious picture hadn't faded from her mind. She wanted to learn more, but it probably wasn't any of her business anyway. Still, it was all such an odd feeling—her reaction to the photo and her sense of knowing the cottage and the people who lived in it.

Slowly, the couple looked at each other with sadness in their faces. They seemed to read Savannah's mind.

Cecilia spoke. "That picture in the hallway is of our daughter and her family. It was taken five years ago." She plucked a tissue to blow her nose before she continued. "It was only months before we found out that our Charlotte had a terminal disease. We lost her later that year. Our grandson and his father live nearby, in town." She pointed next to the mantel. "That old family picture was taken the day we had our first Fourth of July party here at the cottage. And the other is our grandson at three years old, blowing a kiss to his mother as she was taken to the hospital . . . She never came home."

John covered Cecilia's hand with his, and they both looked out to the ever-changing tide.

Once again, an overwhelming sadness overcame Savannah. Perhaps she had sensed from these photos that Charlotte, their daughter, had died. Yet there was something else. Something more.

Without a word, Savannah rose to her feet and walked to the mantel to look more closely at the photo of their young grandson. Those eyes—so big and dark. And that black hair.

"JJ!" she exclaimed with a gasp.

It all came together in an instant. Jonathon Jessup—like Jessup Jonas. And that man in the picture in the hallway. Of course—it was Jonas!

John and Cecilia stared at her in surprise.

"You know JJ, our grandson?" Cecilia asked.

"Yes!" she replied. "I met him and Jonas today. It was the strangest thing."

She returned to the table to tell them of the odd accident that had brought her to Abemly Shores and into JJ and Jonas's life. John and Cecilia could hardly believe the tale.

"Come to think of it, both Jonas and JJ mentioned the loss of Charlotte," Savannah said softly.

At the sound of Charlotte's name, a wave of sadness washed over all three of them. Outside, the wind made a swirling sound and lightly blew through the window near the piano, achieving a delicate plink of a chord.

Chapter 12

SAVANNAH AND MAC

August 2006—Los Angeles

SEVERAL MONTHS PASSED AFTER THAT AUSPICIOUS DAY with the flat tire. It was late August, and Savannah was still touring quite a bit. This time, her travels had taken her to Los Angeles. It would be her first performance in LA. She was actually a little nervous. She knew this performance could lead to offers to compose scores for movies, if the right people heard her. She wasn't certain that was what she wanted, but she was willing to see where the path took her.

When she arrived at the airport and walked through the gate, a limo driver waited with a sign featuring the hotel where she was to stay. It was her signal. There was no entourage and no sign with her name. She wanted to keep her arrival quiet.

Considering her popularity, Savannah opted to travel incognito, when possible. She had hoped to arrive quietly to her hotel for a rest before being recognized by her public.

She nodded to the driver, who then took her carry-on and escorted her to baggage to retrieve her other luggage. He then led her to the waiting limo.

On the way to her hotel, the driver pointed out places of interest and drove her past the concert hall where she would perform. At that, her blood pressure rose.

"Oh my gosh! That hall is amazing. How many does it seat?"

They continued to make small talk as the driver suggested Savannah partake in the mimosas and croissants set out on the shelf next to her seat.

As the sights of LA passed by the window, Savannah's mind couldn't help but travel back to a little town far away. Since February, Savannah had found her way to Abemly Shores several times. Whenever she toured, she would stop and visit with the Sillses and the Beckmans on her way back home to Georgia. She and JJ would take walks along the shore, with Jacey on their heels running in and out of the surf. Sometimes they would get a bite to eat at Jonas's Fine Café, and John, Cecilia, and Jonas himself would join them.

Something strange—almost oddly enchanting—happened to Savannah each time she visited. She felt at home in this town. She felt so accepted and, in a way, loved by these new people she had just met yet seemed to have known all her life.

Her visits also often included coffee with Mona and Josie. She was always intrigued with the history of the town and its people. Savannah listened intently to the many stories Mona shared with her.

In the bookstore was a large file of well-preserved news articles about events and happenings from the past. Sometimes when Mona was busy, Savannah would riffle through the files to quench her thirst for the ghosts of her newfound passion. She read about the Sillses and their cottage. She read about Jonas, the athlete, and his much-too-short marriage to Charlotte, the beautiful starry-eyed hometown girl who dreamed of becoming a ballerina.

Once they arrived at the hotel, a bellman took over for the limo driver. He showed Savannah to the check-in area, then took her to her room. When he opened the door, she saw a huge bouquet of flowers on the credenza along with a card.

"Oh, how lovely! These must be from the hotel or the performing arts committee," she said.

She thanked and tipped the bellman, and he went on his way. Savannah took in a whiff of the flowers as she opened the card. It read, "Welcome to LA—I've missed you! I'm here on business and would love to have dinner. Yours always, Mac."

Savannah let out a groan that turned into a growl. "Mac, we have been *done* for months!" she said aloud.

Savannah hadn't even spoken to Mac since their argument in the hotel room after her performance at Carnegie Hall. She thought it should have been clear that she had moved on. But then she thought, *What could be the hurt in two old friends having dinner? Maybe it will bring us some closure.*

Her performance wasn't until the next night, so Savannah decided to take a short nap before she headed out to see some of the sights. But just as she was dozing off, the phone rang. It was Mac.

"Hello, Mac," she said.

Savannah closed her eyes in frustration as Mac immediately launched into his smooth talk. On and on he went about how they should have dinner—for old times' sake, that is.

"Fine!" Savannah finally said just to shut him up. "Pick me up around seven." She hung up without even saying goodbye.

Lying in bed, she tried to rest and not think about the "best-laid plans" she had once had with Mac. Soon she drifted off.

As she slept, she dreamed of that February day when she was so aggravated with Mac, only to then meet JJ and the other wonderful people in that lovely little town. In her dream, Mac tried to erase the people of Abemly Shores from her mind. He tried to drag her away from them and their goodness. He became a horrifying, evil presence, whipping his cape to make them all disappear!

Savannah began thrashing and moaning in her sleep "No, Mac," she said aloud. "*No!*"

At that moment, the window blew open with such a gust that she bolted into a sitting position. But then she felt a soothing breeze circling her clammy body. In her still-semiconscious state, she thought she heard a *hussshhh* as the unsuspected guest circled her again before leaving through the window.

Savannah shuddered, then stilled with peacefulness as she realized she was no longer damp and frightened. She sighed and leaned back on the array of pillows.

Whoa, that was a trip—or maybe I should say a life-altering experience!

Savannah glanced at the clock. She still had a few hours to check out some shops before Mac would pick her up for dinner. She dashed into the bathroom to shower.

Why did she say yes to this dinner? They hadn't spoken in almost six months, yet here he was checking in with her—meaning, trying to get back in her good graces to rekindle the relationship.

"I have to make it clear once and for all that *we* are over!" she declared out loud.

The rest of the afternoon was great. Shopping, browsing, stopping for tea and coffee, people watching—it was all wonderful. She almost forgot the nightmare and dinner date (which, of course, was a nightmare too).

Taking a brief look at her phone for messages, she saw that it was 6:00 p.m. It was time to go back to the hotel and meet Mac.

"Ugh!" she muttered under her breath.

Promptly at 6:45 p.m., there was a knock on the hotel room door. Sighing with disgust, Savannah set down her brush and walked out of the bathroom to open the door.

Just like always—why does he always have to be early? Isn't on time good enough? That drives me crazy! Then she thought, *Wow, I'm in a great mood to start this evening!*

Savannah tried to open the door slowly, but Mac just pushed on in, carrying more flowers and holding something behind his back.

"Hi, Mac," she said, turning away just in time for his kiss to meet her cheek instead of lips.

His grin reeked of sarcasm as he handed her the flowers. "Well, stranger, it's been too long! We need to get reacquainted sooner than later." He handed her the small box he held behind his back. "I hope I'm not late. Traffic is nuts out there tonight. Maybe we should order room service instead of going out."

He cupped his hands on her hips and pulled her toward him. Immediately, she pushed his hands and spun away. As she did, the gift box dropped and opened to display a diamond bracelet in white gold.

"Knock it off, you big galoot! Who do you think you are, prancing in here fifteen minutes early when you know that's my pet peeve, trying to buy me with flowers and bling, and suggesting we get 'cozy' in my room? This is not a date. I am merely going out for dinner, and you, my big blond frisky friend, are buying!"

With that, she tossed a wrap around her shoulders, pushed past him, and strode out the door.

Dinner was actually somewhat enjoyable. Savannah tried her best to keep it as platonic as possible, treating the evening as a chance for two old friends to reminisce. It seemed to be working just fine—that is, until dinner came to an end. After two hours, Savannah insisted it was time for her to go back to her hotel and get some sleep for the upcoming concert.

"Oh, I get it!" Mac said with a twinkle in his eye. "Sure, let's go back to the hotel and maybe have a nightcap or something."

"You're unbelievable!" she snapped as she rose from her seat and reached for her wrap. "I have a big-deal concert tomorrow and need my rest!"

"Aw, come on, hon. I know you still care about me. And . . . you know . . ." He massaged her shoulders as he helped her with her wrap, and he leaned down to nibble at her neck.

Furious, Savannah threw her hands up. It not only sent the wrap sliding to the floor but also sent her clenched fist right into his ear on accident. Her ring caught flesh and sliced it.

People at nearby tables looked over in surprise as the commotion. Trying not to cause more of a scene, Savannah swept up the wrap and whipped it around his neck to hide the bleeding ear.

"It's late, darling," she gushed with a jovial giggle for effect, trying to play it all off. "I think it's time we go!" She hooked her arm through his and led him out.

Once they were outside, she ripped the wrap off his shoulders.

"What were you thinking? I'm sick of having to tell you no, no, *no*! Don't you get it? We broke up six months ago. You cheated on me at least once. You tried to run my life. And you weren't around for support when I needed you. You came whining back that that other woman didn't mean anything, that it was a 'slipup.' That's a bunch of bologna!"

With tears of frustration, Savannah walked briskly to the car and waited impatiently for him to unlock the door.

With his head down, Mac opened the car door for her, walked to his side, got in, and put the keys in the ignition. But before he started the car, he leaned over to take her hand.

"I'm sorry," he said quietly. "I'm sorry for this date gone wrong."

She softened a bit, took his hand in both of hers, and looked at him through a screen of tears.

"Mac, I know you care. Because we have such a long history, you think we should try again to make a relationship work. But I'm sorry. Things have changed for me since the Carnegie Hall concert last February. I've changed. I have a vision, or I should say a feeling, of what my life might be if I can just wait patiently and continue along the path being paved."

She gently gave his fingers a light kiss. A tear dropped to his hand.

"We'd better get back to the hotel and take care of that ear before it gets infected. I'm sorry about that. I really didn't mean to hit you."

Mac chuckled as he started the engine. "I know you didn't mean to hit me. But lady, you sure can pack a punch!" He grabbed a wad of tissue from the glove box and wedged it around his ear for the drive back.

Once at the hotel, Savannah cleaned and bandaged his wound using the small first aid kit she always traveled with. She thanked him for dinner and the visit, then thanked him for the diamond bracelet even though she declined to keep it. They said goodbye, deciding to remain "friends."

With a lump in her throat and shedding a few tears, she finally closed her door—and closed that overlong chapter in the book of her life.

Right then and there, Savannah knew that when it was time to head home from LA, she wouldn't return to Georgia. Rather, she would go *home*. After seeing so much of the Atlantic seacoast—and after shedding herself of her former life with Mac—it wasn't difficult for her to call a small town on the coast of South Carolina her home. Although she happened upon it purely by accident, she had experienced that "I'm home" feeling the moment her Nikes touched Main Street in Abemly Shores.

Savannah settled into her hotel room with a glass of wine. Raising her glass, she toasted gloomy February mornings and flat tires. And Mr. Jonas. Jonas Beckman. Raven-black hair. Mysterious dark eyes. And that strong, squared chin.

Chapter 13

THE THREE MUSKETEERS

August 2006—Abemly Shores

THE FIRST STOP SAVANNAH MADE WAS to see her friend—and soon-to-be neighbor—Mona. The petite woman was delighted, though not surprised, to hear of Savannah's decision to move to Abemly Shores. The two sat down for some tea to celebrate.

"Mmm, Constant Comment," Savannah said as she took in the aroma of the steeping tea. "You know all my favorite things, Mona! You probably think I'm moving to Abemly just so you can spoil me rotten!" She laughed as she dipped her biscotti into her tea. "Now I just have to find housing in this wonderful, quaint town that has hypnotized me. Possibly a place large enough to accommodate a small piano," she said, clenching her hands together with a giggle.

"Well, my dear friend, I think I have the perfect solution for you!" Mona replied with a wink. "My last tenant moved out, so there's an extra room upstairs in this 'quaint' old house, just waiting for you to fill it. Please say yes! Josie and I won't have it any other way."

The poodle barked and nudged at Savannah's leg.

Taking a sip of her tea, Savannah smiled. "Now, how can I turn down such a gracious offer? Hmm . . . but I'm not sure there's room for a piano in that lovely space."

Mona stood up and placed her palms flat on the table. "No problem! Cecilia and John have mentioned many times that they wish you would visit the cottage more often and entertain them with your music. You can use their piano whenever you'd like."

Mona opened a drawer in the kitchen, took out a key, and placed it in Savannah's hand.

"Welcome home, my friend!"

Savannah marveled at Mona's generosity, not to mention John and Cecilia's. She felt so welcomed by these caring people. She knew they were the closest friends, but their full story was something she would learn over time.

Mona Argyle was born and bred in Abemly Shores. Her parents, Jed and Izzy, had met and married in Charleston, and then in 1948, her father accepted the position of postmaster in the lovely little village of Abemly Shores, South Carolina.

They purchased a small house in town so that Jed could walk to work. In less than a year, Jed and Izzy began filling up that little house with children—five, to be exact. However, they planned for four, hoping for two boys and two girls. Ah, the best-laid plans! The first three children were girls. And number four? Well, number four turned out to be four and five—*twin girls*! Mona was number five, with her twin, Mara, only minutes older than she.

Thrilled to have a houseful, Jed and Izzy were truly delighted with their five daughters! The three-bedroom house needed a few alterations, though, such as an additional bathroom for the girls to share. Jed and Izzy had their own bathroom, and the third bedroom was their sanctuary away from the constant chatter of the girls.

Mona and Mara were three years younger than Vera, who was number three and constantly trying to boss her younger sisters around. But as they got older, Vera, the confused "middle child," changed her direction and decided to hang out with the older sisters. This left the twins happy to hang together and find friends their own age.

They took advantage of the fact that they were identical twins, loving to play jokes on people trying to guess which one was which. When they went to school, there was a boy named Johnny Sills who insisted he could tell them apart. They constantly came up with schemes to trick him. The girls and Johnny did everything together. The other kids at school began calling them "the triplets" because they were inseparable. Mara would tell Mona that someday she wanted to marry Johnny and that they'd have five girls, just like their own family. She swore her sister to secrecy.

As the twins got older and started middle school, their relationship with Johnny Sills began to change. He got involved with sports and took up playing the French horn in the school band, which kept him really busy. Being in sports, he started hanging out with Easton Baines and his other teammates, which didn't give him much free time to spend with Mona and Mara Argyle.

Then it happened! At the beginning of seventh grade, a new girl moved to town. Cecilia Rombauer and her family had relocated to Abemly Shores because her dad was the new principal at the high school.

Uh-oh. With Cecilia being the new girl in town, she became very popular, especially with the boys. Right away, Mara was jealous and didn't like this new girl with long, silky blond hair and big brown eyes that seemed to twinkle whenever she saw Johnny Sills.

"*Hmph*! He's *my* Johnny!" Mara crossed her arms over her chest and stomped her feet as she confided in her sister with tears dripping down her face. "I knew him first, and that new girl can't have him! It's just not fair—she can't just march into town and change everything on us!"

"Mara, it's not her fault," Mona insisted. "She doesn't know how things were with the three of us. Besides, she's new and probably misses her old friends. She probably feels alone here. She actually seems kind of nice. When I dropped my lunch tray on Tuesday after Easton Baines bumped into me on purpose, she was the only one who came over to help me clean up the mess."

Mona hesitated, on alert, to watch Mara's reaction. She was prepared to duck if Mara threw something at her during her tantrum.

"Mona! I can't believe you're on her side. We're twins, and we need to stick together!" Once again, she stomped her feet, this time while giving her sister the evil eye. "If you're going to be her friend, then . . . then . . ." She let out a big sigh. "Then you are not my friend *anymore*!"

She ran off and locked herself in the bathroom shared by all five girls. (Though it didn't last long, once the three older girls came home from school.)

Mara stayed angry until Reginald Sands started hanging around, waiting to walk her home after school. The nights they had glee club together really made her happy because they would stop at the ice cream shop, where Reg often treated her to a cone. Sometimes Mona and Easton would join them for ice cream—once Mona realized Easton was constantly teasing her because he really liked her. They actually became quite an item.

Through high school, Easton was the football hero and team captain, and Mona became his personal cheerleader. They were rarely seen apart, and it was a given that they would someday marry and raise their family in Abemly Shores. Easton and John were best buddies. Easton supported John's love of music, even though he didn't partake in the venue.

Mona and John remained good friends and were still part of "the triplets." However, one thing had changed—the third triplet's name was Cecilia.

Cecilia Rombauer was a very special girl. All you had to do was just ask her two best friends, John and Mona. She was a gifted pianist already at age thirteen and loved to sew, which wasn't surprising in that her mother was a meticulous seamstress. Cecilia was smart, pretty, and tall with dancer's legs that went on forever. Aside from her talents, she was well liked by everyone because she was such a nice, caring person. Even Mara made amends with her, but it helped to have Reginald by her side.

During their high school years, the trio of John, Cecilia, and Mona stuck together through thick and thin. Although Mona didn't play an instrument, she had a beautiful singing voice. The three of them put a musical group together, calling themselves the Three Musketeers. The group managed to make a little money performing for local events and sometimes parties or even an occasional wedding.

After graduation, John and Cecilia left for college to continue their music studies. John also pursued a degree in education. Mona, on the other hand, stayed home and took business classes at the community college in a nearby town. She had always dreamed of someday opening a bookshop. With a business background, she would be able to run it on her own. This became her quest while waiting for the love of her life, Easton, to return from his tour of duty in the army. He chose to enlist shortly after graduation. He planned to continue his schooling and marry Mona when he returned.

Mara accepted Reginald's proposal, and they married. Shortly after their wedding, they started a family of their own. So with four of the Argyle girls out of the house—either married or away at college—Jed and Izzy decided to sell their house in town, seeing as retirement was creeping up on them. They bought a little bungalow near the beach. When they discussed their plans with Mona, she asked if they would allow her to rent-to-own the house she had grown up in. Her parents were thrilled to keep the house in the family and were even more excited when she explained her plans to turn the front rooms into a bookstore and live upstairs.

John and Cecilia moved back to Abemly Shores after graduating from college. They married shortly thereafter. Of course, Mona was standing next to the bride as the young couple promised to love and honor and cherish one another all the days of their lives. After the vows were spoken, Mona turned to face them and sang "Cherish." John had always told Cecilia how he cherished her.

A few months later, John and Cecilia were driving back from a particularly romantic afternoon at the beach when they came upon a winding gravel road lined with trees. Looking at each other, they decided on an adventure. They parked the car and hand in hand meandered down the path with trees forming a canopy to shield them from the hot sun. There was a bend along the path. When they took the turn, both had to stop and take time to catch their breath.

A deserted cottage stood two stories high with shuttered windows and remnants of a flower garden in hibernation, waiting for the loving touch of the perfect green thumb. Their eyes moved from the garden to a magnificent covered porch looking very much like the deck of a ship contemplating the canvas of blue ocean at its bow. They knew in their heart of hearts that this was to be their home, where they would live and love always.

Nine months later, to the day, a baby was born. Her name was Charlotte.

Chapter 14

SAVANNAH AND JONAS: A LOVE STORY

Fall 2006—Abemly Shores

SAVANNAH DROVE SLOWLY THROUGH the magical town of Abemly Shores, her new home. In a few short weeks, it had imprinted upon her so many hopes and dreams. She took photographs in her mind of the tree-lined boulevard, the many quaint shops, the charming brick sidewalks, and the kind and caring people she met while exploring this cozy world.

Warm and welcoming Mona was Savannah's new best friend. They spent hours together, with Savannah asking questions and Mona teaching her about the town's history and the comings and goings of its people. And then there were John and Cecilia Sills and their heartwarming, magnificent cottage by the water. Savannah and Mona often met the couple for lunch, usually at Jonas's Fine Café.

It was all Savannah could do not to drool whenever Jonas took their order. Yes, you could say she had it bad! Those amazing, hypnotic eyes of Jonas Beckman—she just couldn't get him out of her mind. She kept seeing that dimpled smile glowing amidst all that shiny black hair under his cap.

I need to stop doing this to myself! Savannah would think, shaking his vision from her head. But she'd already fallen for him—hook, line, and sinker.

Unfortunately, though, Jonas didn't seem to feel the same about her. Savannah remembered the time at the café when Jonas introduced her to his friend Cassie, a very attractive little blonde picking up coffee for her coworkers. Jonas and Cassie appeared to have a close friendship but nothing more.

If a woman like Cassie can't get his full attention, then I don't know why he'd give me the time of day, Savannah told herself. *Wouldn't you know I'd fall for someone who has no interest in ever falling in love again?*

Then again, Savannah wondered if Cassie was only interested in friendship too. Savannah thought she was pleasant, but there was something sad about her—something about her demeanor. Or maybe she was just one of those people who kept to themselves. Savannah hoped she would get to know Cassie better—perhaps Cassie could use another friend.

As enthralled as Savannah was with Jonas, JJ was actually her "main man." Sweet, lovable JJ and his "mixed-up" poodle. She was so taken by that little boy. The moment she first saw those dark eyes peering out at her, he had her in the palm of his hand. There wasn't anything she wouldn't do for him.

Savannah often swung by the café to pick up JJ for special outings. Each time, they encouraged Jonas to join them, but he always said he wasn't "available." So Savannah and JJ would go visit his grandparents. One of their favorite pastimes was walking the beach and picking up shells. Sometimes, they'd sit on the porch and create picture frames out of the shells they'd found. Other times, they played games or read together, and they often loved to spend time at that beautiful piano.

As it turned out, Savannah's connection with JJ eventually paved the way for a connection with his father. Each time Savannah came by to scoop up JJ for their outings, Jonas became more entangled in her many attributes. Her knowing hazel eyes would constantly catch him off guard whenever she smiled. Whenever she turned to walk away, he wished he could touch the long auburn curls that tickled her shoulders when she moved or laughed—yes, that laugh that was as melodic as her music.

Over the months, Jonas grew more and more comfortable with Savannah, which took lots of patience on her part. But it was worth the wait. Before long, Jonas was suddenly "available" to join JJ and Savannah on their outings.

One evening, Mona was getting ready to close the bookstore when Savannah walked in.

"Mona, dinner is on me tonight. I'm heading to the café to get some takeout, then I'll head back here so we can watch TV and just chill."

"That sounds wonderful," Mona replied. "I'm exhausted from this busy day and would love to sit for a bit. I'll finish closing while you get the food!"

Savannah walked into the café and smiled at the waitress. "Hi, Sandy. Is my order ready for take—"

But before she could finish the sentence, Jonas suddenly appeared right next to her. There was something different about him—he seemed as shy and nervous as a schoolboy.

"Hey, Savannah. How are things? Um, JJ is upstairs doing homework . . . and . . . I . . . was thinking . . . would you maybe like to catch a movie or dinner . . . sometime?" Then he quickly added, "Soon? Just the two of us? Perhaps?"

Just then, the waitress handed Savannah her order, but Savannah couldn't even command her fingers to grasp the bag. Without Jonas's quick reflexes, the food would have been all over that lovely pine floor.

Savannah was in total shock at Jonas's offer. She tried to play it cool, but a loud *"Absolutely yes!"* came out of her mouth before she even realized it.

Both Savannah and Jonas burst into laughter.

As Jonas walked Savannah to the café door, he touched her arm, sliding his hand down to take hers and give it a light squeeze.

"Then I'll pick you up tomorrow, seven-ish. And we'll create our evening from there," he added with a wink of those amazing black eyes.

Savannah was melting as she made her way up the street to Book Benders. Poor Mona was probably starving by now, waiting for her to return with dinner. In fact, when Savannah stepped inside, Mona was ready to ask what took so long—but then she saw Savannah's face and immediately had her answer.

Mona smiled slyly and clapped her hands together. "Well, it's about time you two figured out how to get together," she announced. "So, where's he taking you? Not that it matters. It's just good that you're doing something together!"

At seven-ish Saturday night, the doorbell rang. Savannah opened the door for Jonas to begin their first date. He stood on the stoop holding a bouquet of lilies. As he handed them to her, he bent down to kiss her cheek.

Once again, she was melting, melting right into his arms. He was so sweet and polite, making her feel as if she were on her first high school date.

Jonas took her hand, then peeked into the house. "Mona, no need to wait up—I promise I'll have her back at a reasonable time!" he called out with that infectious laugh of his.

And off they went.

Following up a light meal and movie, they went to the ice cream shop on Main Street. They strolled along the boulevard, holding hands and looking at the charming old homes. They eventually went behind Jonas's Fine Café and across the big lawn to Waterfront Park. They sat on a bench looking out to Abemly Sound, enjoying the warm breeze that embraced them with her dance, affirming their happiness. They talked about everything under the sun, and when they thought there was no more to share, they talked more.

Savannah knew she'd never forget how he took her hand in his and brought it to his lips. The kiss felt like a soft feather blowing by. Then those wonderful, mysterious eyes asked if he could kiss her. She leaned in to accept the much-awaited gift. Soft and warm, his lips on hers, the fit was so perfect. Together like this—everything was right with the world.

From that night on, they were inseparable. Sometimes when Jonas wasn't working, he would come by the house to sit in the rocker on the porch and listen to her music. Their courtship was like something out of a romance novel, with never-ending walks on the beach holding hands, warm kisses, and always much laughter shared. Oh, and the flowers! He always brought her flowers, whether it was a large bouquet or a single mum he picked himself. In his oh-so reserved manner, he possessed more kindness and love than anyone she'd ever known.

And then on a beautiful day in late October 2007, with the sun beginning to set and a gentle breeze off the ocean, Jonas and Savannah became husband and wife. They recited their vows near the same Waterfront Park bench where they had shared their first kiss and where he had proposed to her only months before.

Friends and family shared the special occasion with them. Jonas asked JJ to be his best man and Nathan, his brother-in-law, to be the groomsman. Savannah's sister, Adrianna, was her matron of honor. As it turned out, Cassie and Savannah had become good friends, and she agreed to be a bridesmaid. They also ended up with two ring bearers and two flower girls, considering there was no way to choose only one of each. So, JJ's cousins were thrilled to be ring bearers (or "junior grooms-men") in their dapper mini suits, while Adrianna's girls looked like Disney princesses in their special handmade dresses, each carrying a basket of lilies.

Everyone was so full of smiles! The very special music consisted of a reunion of the Three Musketeers, which of course included John with his French horn, Cecilia on JJ's keyboard, and Mona singing. As the couple exchanged rings, Mona began singing "Cherish," which Savannah and Jonas had chosen as an echo from Cecilia and John's nuptials.

Just then, the oddest thing happened. Savannah started to tear up, so Jonas reached for the hankie from his breast pocket. As he pulled it out, something fell from the hankie to the ground.

He looked down to see a small round white object. A stone. Jonas bent down to retrieve it. As he stood back up and studied the stone in his hand, he went pale as a ghost and broke into a sweat.

But then, instantly, a miraculous cool breeze swirled around him, soothing and cooling the very sweat off Jonas. His color came back immediately. There was something in the air, something in the wind. Some calm that promoted comfort. He wasn't sure exactly what it was, but he had felt it so strongly.

Even Savannah seemed to feel it. She had noticed Jonas pick up a stone of some sort, then she noticed that wonderful breeze. She smiled at him, somewhat perplexed.

With that smooth stone hidden in his grasp, Jonas took Savannah's hand. Now they held the smooth stone together.

After they were pronounced husband and wife and they kissed, Jonas guided Savannah to the edge of the water, still holding hands. Jonas took their clasped hands in his other hand and brought them to his lips. He gazed into her eyes.

"I love you," he said.

Then he tossed the stone to the ocean, watching it skip three times before disappearing into the never-ending darkness of the water.

Savannah looked at him, questioning, though she knew it made total sense to him.

He just looked back into those hazel eyes he had grown to know so well. All he said was, "Full circle."

He hugged her, and they shared a long and sensual kiss. They forgot they had an audience—until people began applauding and hooting and hollering.

Before the couple left for their honeymoon in Aspen, JJ expressed his worry about them going off alone to the wilds of Colorado. They assured him that Aspen wasn't too wild—unless they came across a bear while hiking. Before JJ could react to this news, Jonas quickly explained how they could avoid a bear encounter or deal with one, if need be.

Satisfied with this answer, JJ nodded. "Okay. That checks out. I can let you guys go."

The honeymoon was glorious, romantic, and magical! It was just the two of them—so mesmerized by each other and so much in love—in what must be one of the most beautiful places on earth.

They stayed at an inn not far from the base of Aspen Mountain. The accommodations were so cozy and romantic, with a large wood-burning fireplace in the bedroom as well as the living room. The aroma of the wood smoke journeying up the chimney was enchanting.

French doors led from the bedroom out to an inviting balcony facing the mountain. Evenings were cool, and they loved to open the balcony doors to allow the hypnotizing mountain air to entertain the senses. Beautiful nights were shared in the huge four-poster bed with its soft featherbed mattress. The abundant down comforter harbored the lovers from the cool air.

The brisk morning breeze would then travel through their room to alert them of a new day, gently rustling the love cocoon they'd spun the night before. Every day, they shared breakfast on the balcony with the sun warming their faces as they looked at the unparalleled beauty of the mountain.

They would then plan out the day ahead, which consisted of everything from a hike through Maroon Bells, a walk or bike ride along the river, a jeep ride into Snowmass, shopping in the quaint stores, or a romantic gondola ride and lunch up at the top of the breathtaking mountain.

One of the more special memories was visiting the John Denver Sanctuary and walking amidst the awe-inspiring boulders inscribed with his name and many lyrics from his songs. It was such a peaceful arena, with beautiful, fragrant flowers and the quiet, calming sound of the Roaring Fork River beside the Rio Grande Trail.

Jonas and Savannah said farewell to Aspen—with the enticing scent of mountain air and precious memories lingering behind them. It was time to begin their life together back home in Abemly Shores.

A few months later, in February, JJ came running into the café with his dark eyes sparkling and a great big smile.

"Mom! Can you believe it? I'll be ten years old in just two days!" Taking a deep breath, he grinned and took a cookie from the jar on the counter.

Standing in front of the bar during the lunch rush, Savannah smirked. "So why are you so excited about your tenth birthday? It wouldn't have anything to do with the fact that once you're ten, you can officially work at the café, would it?"

What a great kid, she thought and hugged him tight. *How many ten-year-old boys wished for their birthday just so they could start busing tables?* JJ was quite ecstatic at the opportunity.

"What a very special little boy I've been blessed with!" Savannah spoke out loud as she wiped a tear from her eye.

Still living in the cozy apartment above the café, the Beckman family took advantage of the fact that they were closed on Sundays and held his birthday party downstairs. JJ insisted on serving the food himself.

There was quite the JJ fan club at the party. Aside from three sets of proud grandparents and numerous aunts, uncles, and cousins, he had invited his best friend, Joey Sands, and two other boys. He had also sent a special invite to Mona and Josie.

JJ also wanted to play piano for his guests on his keyboard, so when Jonas brought in the cake, JJ played while everyone sang "Happy Birthday to You." What a wonderful day that was—and a very long one!

That night when Jonas and Savannah tucked him into bed, they asked if he'd gotten everything he wished for.

"I'm excited about all my presents," he replied, "but there's something I have wished for, for a long time . . . and that's a brother or sister of my very own."

He searched his parents' eyes with a smile. At that moment, a single leaf danced through the open window, swirling with the breeze until it gracefully perched on Savannah's shoulder. Jonas put his arm around her and gently lifted the leaf from her shoulder. It gave off a light hint of honeysuckle.

Savannah took a deep breath and replied with a smile, "Hmm . . ."

Chapter 15
AN ADDITION

Fall 2008—Abemly Shores

In September, John and Cecilia moved to a condo on the edge of town, deciding it would be easier for them to have a smaller space. Because Jonas and Savannah had always loved the cottage by the shore and because JJ felt so connected to it, they bought it and moved in that fall.

Shortly after, Savannah headed out on the road for a short tour in the Midwest. Before the end of the weeklong trip, she started feeling ill. Calling from her hotel bed, she shared her discomfort with Mona.

"I'm not the most pleasant patient when I'm sick, you know," Savannah said. "I'm usually pretty healthy, so I can't tolerate colds and the flu at all! I think it's all because of being on the road like this. You know I don't enjoy touring like I used to."

"I understand how you feel and why you aren't as thrilled to tour these days," Mona interjected. "But I really think you should visit the doctor once you get home. She may be able to prescribe something to help get you back on your feet."

"Thank you for caring, Mona. And yes, I will see the doc if this doesn't go away soon. Well, I better get myself off to the piano to work on my new jazz piece. I'll catch up with you once I'm home."

In a few days, Savannah was thrilled to be back home, sleeping in her own bed with Jonas's arms around her. She felt the sun coming through the bedroom window, and she smiled as she touched the warm arms surrounding her. She opened her eyes and turned toward Jonas to say good morning.

Suddenly, she flung those arms wrapping her in a loving embrace. She covered her mouth with cupped hands and almost fell out of bed trying to beeline it to the bathroom. Flipping up the toilet seat just in time, she spewed up everything she'd consumed from the welcome-home dinner her guys had prepared the night before. What a disaster!

Poor Jonas came out of calming dreams to all this hysteria. He tried to jump out of bed so fast that he got tangled up in the sheets and ended up taking a dive onto his knees. What a sight he was, running in to check on Savannah with the sheet still wrapped around his legs and one knee scraped and bleeding.

"What in the world? You scared me to death! Are you okay?" Jonas spit out the words as he hobbled into the bathroom and grabbed a wad of tissue to dab at his bloody knee.

Savannah was hovering over the toilet wearing only Jonas's T-shirt. She turned to look at the adorable, unfortunate, disheveled guy. Even through her pale, perspiring face, she couldn't help but choke out a few good laughs.

"Oh my gosh—just look at us!" She stood up and transferred her aching body to the sink to clean up a bit. "I'm okay. Actually, I'm beginning to feel a little better these days—and a few pounds lighter to boot," she said with a grin.

Just as she started brushing her teeth, she felt hands at her waist. With a mouthful of toothpaste, she eyed Jonas through the mirror, then smiled as he rested his chin on her shoulder and gave her a playful wink. She rinsed the last bit of toothpaste from her lips.

"Are you kidding me? I'm a mess!"

"We both need to shower, don't we?" Then with a pout, he looked down at his bruised knee, followed by a wink.

"It's interesting how all of a sudden my 'flu' has passed. I'm most obliged to take you up on your offer." She winked back at him with a sly grin.

Even though Savannah thought she was on the mend, she had a repeat bathroom performance the next day when the sun began to peek through the window. Savannah hated being sick, and Jonas was getting more and more concerned. They agreed she should make an appointment to see Dr. McAira.

So on a glorious, rainy day in November—the Monday before Thanksgiving—Dr. McAira revealed the cause for Savannah's symptoms. The Jonas Beckman family would be welcoming a new baby in early July 2009.

"*Pregnant?*" shrieked Savannah. "But . . . I . . . we . . . oh my goodness!" She jumped to her feet, doing a little jig. "Yes! Yes! Jonas and I are having a baby—a beautiful, wonderful baby—together!"

Driving home from the appointment, Savannah sang to herself as she anticipated sharing the news with Jonas, then JJ. "Having a baby! Having his baby!"

Heading up the tree-lined drive, she tapped gleefully on the steering wheel in time with the music. As the house came into view, she spotted Jonas leaning against the railing of the porch, tossing a coin in the air. He took the stairs in twos toward the car once she parked.

"Hey, what did the doc say? Are you going to give us all the flu? 'Cuz you know I can't afford to be sick, especially going into our busy holiday season at the café."

Jonas opened the door and gave her a tentative peck on the cheek, afraid of whatever germs she might be carrying. As she climbed out of the car, Savannah doubled over as if she would be sick—but then she grinned ear to ear.

"It's okay to kiss me full on the lips," she said. She puckered up and fluttered her eyelashes at him. "Jonas, my love, don't worry about me being contagious—you can't possibly catch what I have." She took his hand in hers and placed it on her belly.

"Hon, what in the heck are you talking about? Of course the flu is contag—"

He suddenly stopped midsentence. He stared at the hand he held against her stomach, then into her eyes.

"Ah, yes," Savannah said while Jonas stared in shock. "Dr. McAira said what I have will last until, oh, sometime in the beginning of July!"

Then she squealed as Jonas lifted her off the ground in a big but gentle bear hug.

"Are you serious? Do you mean we're . . . pregnant . . . having a . . . *B-A-B-Y*? I mean, like, our baby?"

He set her solidly back on the ground, then kneeled down to be eye level with her belly. As he touched her belly lightly with his hands, he whispered, "I love you, little one," and kissed her tummy.

Laughing, Savannah said, "So, shall we take this inside and share the good news with our son?"

Together, Jonas and Savannah headed into the kitchen, where JJ was working on the dough for Thanksgiving cookies. He glanced up nervously as they walked in. He had been worried about Savannah's appointment.

Jonas let out a sigh and looked into his son's concerned eyes. "Well, your mom and I have something to tell you . . ." He paused for dramatic tension. "We hope you won't mind sharing us with your new brother or sister!"

Immediately, JJ started jumping and dancing around the room. "Hooray! I'm going to be a big brother!"

Flour from his hands went flying as he continued his jubilance about the room. Poor Jacey didn't know what to think of her best friend. She began barking and spinning in circles. JJ took hold of Jacey's paws and did a little dance with her.

"Jacey, you're going to have another friend in the house—woo-hoo!"

Jacey replied with two yips.

Of course, JJ had a million questions. He ran back and forth between Jonas and Savannah with each one.

"So, when will my brother be born? Would it be okay if I make a list of names? I'm okay if he stays in my room 'cuz he'll be scared to be alone. I'll teach him to play softball and take him to football games and movies!"

"Hang on, handsome," Savannah chimed in when JJ paused to take a breath. "What if this 'brother' of yours turns out to be a little sister? Hmm?"

At first, they were a bit concerned about his reaction. He looked very surprised and pensive for a few minutes. But then he started right up again. JJ's speech increased in speed as he imagined life with a little sister.

"A sister—oh, wow! Well, I'll take really good care and watch out for her. I'll take her on walks in her stroller. And when she's a little bigger, we can walk together to the ice cream shop. And I'll be sure to always hold her hand and watch out when we cross the street. I could build her a dollhouse. And I guess I'd even pretend to like playing with her. I'd let her serve me tea at her tea parties. Of course, when she gets older, I'd make sure she only went out on dates with really nice guys. I might even have to go with them the first few times." Without skipping a beat, he added, "No matter what the baby is, I'm going to teach it to play piano and maybe even how to dance."

"Holy smokes, dude," Jonas said as he rustled JJ's black hair. "You are going to be an extremely busy big brother!"

Grinning, JJ announced, "I'm going to my room to make lists of girls' and boys' names. Come on, Jacey—you can help."

Before he left the kitchen, though, he turned back to Savannah and hugged her.

"If it's a girl, I hope she looks just like you, 'cuz then she'll be beautiful!"

Next, he walked toward Jonas and gave him a bear hug.

"And if it's a boy baby, I want him to look just like 'us men.'"

When JJ left the room, his parents looked with bewilderment into each other's eyes. Jonas put his arms around Savannah.

"We are so lucky!" he said as he kissed her.

At that moment, JJ bounced back around the corner to peek into the kitchen. "Would it be okay if I make an announcement at Thanksgiving dinner about the new baby? And oh yeah, one more thing—it doesn't really matter to me what the baby is. I'll always love it and take care of it! No matter what." He reached his arms around both of them. "I'm *so* excited about our new baby!"

As if they couldn't already tell.

As excited as JJ was to share their news, you would have thought Thanksgiving was really Christmas. The day was just cool enough to have a welcoming fire in both the kitchen and the living room. Between the wood smoke and the tantalizing scents coming from the kitchen, everyone was already smiling. They were looking forward to a wonderful family day watching the Macy's parade on TV, enjoying a delightful meal, and, naturally, watching football.

Harold and Dorothy Sheridan—along with John, Cecilia, and Mona—were more interested in watching the musical productions in the Macy's parade. Meanwhile, JJ, Jonas, and Steve and Shelly Beckman were more interested in cheering on the football teams. Thankfully, Uncle Nathan, Aunt Sylvie, and their boys were able to keep the group on an even keel, managing sports and music harmoniously.

Anticipation of the announcement was almost too much for JJ. He made special place cards for each guest. On each card, he wrote that person's relationship to the newest Beckman, then enclosed it in an envelope and put it on the table. No one was to open them until they were all seated for the meal.

Once all were ready, JJ counted to three, and the guests opened their envelopes. The excitement of the moment was too much to take.

With tears in her eyes, Cecilia kissed Savannah on the cheek. "I'm so very happy for you both!" she exclaimed.

The rest of that day was nothing but laughter, happiness, and good thoughts for all the Beckmans, their extended family, and their special friends.

After a wonderful celebration, the Jonas Beckman family—with Jacey, of course—stood on the porch to thank their guests for coming and wish them safe travels. When everyone drove off, the three of them lingered on the porch and listened to the surf.

Oddly, an atypical wind for the time of year wrapped her sultry warmth across the porch and swept around them. They watched her swirl, gathering fallen oak leaves, drawing them toward the sky . . . making way for the new.

The months passed quickly. Before they knew it, it was summer. They had decided not to find out the sex of the baby until it was born. The due date was July 1, which had them wondering if they would have a firecracker baby on the Fourth of July.

That particular Independence Day was predicted to be almost one hundred degrees before sunset. Fortunately, a pleasant breeze came off the ocean, helping it feel more like eighty-five than one hundred.

Nevertheless, friends and family were invited to the barbecue and fireworks party at the cottage. Over the years, John and Cecilia had hosted this annual event for everyone to gather, eat, and be merry. And now Jonas and Savannah were excited to carry on the tradition.

But when people began arriving in the early afternoon, they were surprised to see Savannah in her still-very-pregnant state sitting in a lawn chair in front of a kiddie pool. As Cassie came over for a hug, Savannah gave Jonas a side-glance, appearing a bit annoyed.

"So, Cassie," Savannah said, "I suppose you agree with my dear husband that I'm to do nothing but be the designated babysitter and pool tester today. Jonas came up with the idea that I have to sit here and keep my feet cool in the pool."

Rolling her eyes, she blew a kiss Jonas's way. Then she turned back to Cassie.

"But you, my friend, can sit with me and help oversee any issues with the children. Then I don't have to play lifeguard." She giggled and splashed water with her foot.

What a wonderful day! Even with the heat, everyone was having a great time with croquet tournaments, three-legged races, and water balloon tosses (or you might call them water balloon fights). Horseshoes proved to be serious competition, and the bridge ladies set up tables on the porch, shielding themselves from the hot sun. As the day shifted into evening, cooking took precedence. The grill masters and assistant grill masters decided to have a cook-off. The fun never stopped.

When the fire pit got stoked up for marshmallows, Savannah couldn't just sit with her feet in the pool and be waited on any longer. She pushed herself out of her chair.

"Being the s'mores queen, I must do it myself!" she announced.

She carefully worked to perfectly bronze her marshmallow and artfully blow out the flame whenever it became too hot. Everyone enjoyed the peaceful moment.

That is, until Savannah screamed "My water broke!" right there in front of all their family and friends. Immediately she turned a bright shade of red, realizing all eyes were on her.

JJ became quite upset—if not confused—that his mom was shouting and suddenly wet.

"Hey! Who threw a water balloon at my mom?" He jumped up and looked around for the guilty party. "That was mean—she's going to have a baby soon!" He shook his fist at the group.

But when Savannah doubled over in pain, JJ began shouting. "Dad! Come quick—help! Mom needs help! Someone threw a balloon at her. She's all wet and in pain! *Help*!"

Jonas was already at Savannah's side. He put one arm around her and the other around JJ. "Hey, bud, it's going to be all right. No one hurt your mom or threw a balloon at her. She's just ready to have your brother or sister now. It's time for me to take her to the hospital."

At that moment, JJ had a flashback of his dad and a blond woman named Charlotte. His mother. His first mother. One day, his dad said he was taking her to the hospital. JJ blew her a kiss for her to hold until she returned home.

"No, Dad!" JJ cried. "You can't take her to the hospital—what if she doesn't come home, just like Mom Charlotte?" With tears in his eyes, he ran to hold on to Savannah. "Don't go, Mom. Please don't go."

"JJ, sweetie—listen to me," Savannah said, wincing and holding her stomach. "I will be just fine, and so will the baby. We will be one big happy family. I promise." Smiling, she squeezed his hands and kissed him on the cheek. "But Dad and I have to go, or this baby might be born right here!"

They left for the hospital with Dr. McAira, who just happened to be a guest at the party. John and Cecilia agreed to look after the guests and take care of cleanup, while Mona and JJ car-avanned after the others to the hospital. Once at the hospital, JJ paced the hallway, wearing a rut in the floor.

Then at 11:55 p.m. on July 4, Jonas appeared in the hall-way with a glowing smile. JJ looked up at him with questioning eyes.

"JJ, Mom would like to see you and introduce you to a special someone." Jonas winked at Mona and signaled to her to join them.

Wide-eyed, JJ smiled at his dad and followed him to Savannah's birthing suite. Hesitantly, he glanced around. Savannah was on a bed, radiant and happy, with a small pink bundle in her arms.

Jonas guided JJ to the couch. Jonas gently picked up the bundle from Savannah's arms and placed it carefully in JJ's arms.

"JJ, say hello to your little sister, Lily Marie."

Gazing lovingly at his sister, JJ said, "I love you so much, little Lily. I'll always look out for you." He leaned down to the baby and very gently kissed the top of her head.

Mona took a seat beside JJ, putting her arm around him. With tears in her eyes, she stroked the baby's cheek.

Lily began to whimper, so Jonas picked up his beautiful new daughter and placed her back in Savannah's arms. A gentle breeze caused the window to rattle, then a light pitter-patter of rain wished those inside love. It was a truly precious moment.

Part Two

Chapter 16

THAT FEELING

April 12, 2012—Abemly Shores

FOR SAVANNAH, THE SOUND OF BIRDS CHIRPING and the surf rolling on a warm breeze was the best way to be wakened. She turned to her side, using her hands as a pillow so she could take in the rising sun through the curtains gently moving in the breeze. She nestled under the double-wedding-ring quilt she had come to cherish in the six years since she first saw it on the cottage porch.

She heard the delicate click-click of dog paws up and down the hall. Jacey was checking for life in the other bedrooms.

"It's just you and me today," she called out to the whining dog.

Jonas had taken JJ and Lily on an overnight fishing and camping trip with Uncle Nathan and the twins. They would be home the next morning. The days for Savannah to be home alone were few and far between. However much Savannah loved being with her family, there was just something special about having her own time to compose music and reflect on her life.

"How about I throw on some clothes and we'll go for a run?" Savannah offered.

In an instant, Jacey ran into the room, jumped on the bed, then began her ballet spinning.

"Okay, okay! Let's go!" Savannah said with a laugh.

Savannah dressed for a run, then headed downstairs. It was a gorgeous spring day—maybe a bit brisk. But that made it perfect for running on the beach. She wasn't sure how cool it would be by the water, so she grabbed a sweatshirt off the coatrack and tied it around her waist.

As soon as Savannah opened the porch door, Jacey ran out to check for the most recent smells in the garden, then ran back and began her spinning dance again. Savannah laughed and tossed a Frisbee in the air, which Jacey caught on a spin. Realizing the air was a bit chilly after all, Savannah wrapped the sweatshirt around her shoulders, then off they went to run and play along the shoreline.

After a three-mile run and many games of Frisbee, it was time to head back. The two had earned their breakfast. As they walked toward home, Jacey ran in and out of the waves with the Frisbee in her mouth. But then she dropped the Frisbee and scooped up something apparently more interesting.

"What do you have there?" Savannah asked.

Whatever Jacey had clenched in her teeth was small. Savannah couldn't see it. She picked up the Frisbee and tossed it, hoping it would be a fair trade for the object Jacey had found.

Before she leaped to retrieve the flying disc, Jacey released whatever she had been so enamored with. Savannah bent down to examine it.

It was an ordinary white stone—yet not so ordinary at all. It was flat with perfectly rounded edges. It also had an odd jagged hairline crack down the center. When she held the stone up to the sun, the jagged line almost appeared to have a slight pink cast.

Jacey came running back with the Frisbee, though she looked longingly at the stone Savannah now held.

"So you think there's something special about this stone, hmm?"

Savannah rubbed it between her fingers. It was very smooth. She thought it was amazing how the ocean water could sculpt something so perfectly.

Savannah pulled her sweatshirt fully on now to keep from getting a chill after the run. She slipped the white stone into her pocket. While they finished their walk back to the house, she slipped her hand into her pocket and kept stroking the tiny jagged line on the stone. She wondered why she felt the need to bring the stone home, to the cottage.

Reaching the edge of the tree-lined road, Savannah paused for a moment to catch her breath and take in the beauty of the house. Heading toward the porch, she bent down to pick a few early flowers from the garden.

Exhilarated and starving, both Savannah and Jacey were ready for breakfast. Jacey of course spun in circles to earn her food. Savannah then prepared her own meal of poached eggs and Canadian bacon with homemade toast and jam—and last but not least, a pot of coffee.

She sat down at the round kitchen table to enjoy her breakfast and look over her latest jazz composition. She anticipated being perched at the piano with the ocean breeze blowing through her hair for hours on end. In a few days, she would leave for a two-week West Coast tour. There was much to do in the meantime.

After several hours of practicing and working on her newest piece, she got up to stretch and take a break. She went to the kitchen and poured an iced tea, which she took out to the porch to entertain her senses.

The air was so fragrant from the blooming flowers. The smell of the freshly mowed lawn was intoxicating. And the sound of the surf was always enchanting—it never got old. Savannah smiled as she realized Jacey had followed her out to the porch and was settling down to sunbathe on the steps.

"You're such a good friend to have around!" Savannah told her.

Jacey didn't look up but wagged her tail, acknowledging the compliment.

"Oh, I love it here so much!" Savannah said aloud.

She almost hated to leave for her tour. But as long as she knew she'd soon return to their little paradise, all would be fine. Sighing, she took a long sip of the tea, then returned to the piano, leaving Jacey to sleep in the sun.

Many hours later, Savannah stood up again from the piano, this time to call it a day. Her neck and shoulders were stiff.

She knew just the remedy.

"*Ahh!*" Savannah moaned as she eased herself into the warmth of the bubbling water in the tub. Almost immediately, she felt soothing comfort. She massaged the sore muscles beneath her tender, naked flesh.

As she adjusted herself in the tub, she thought of the exhausting days of touring that would follow. Quickly, she whisked the worries from her mind. Now it was time to relax and take in the sweet, mellow scent of the magnolia candle perched on the small table next to the claw-foot tub. She watched the flame dance as the breeze through the open window kissed it, producing a gray ghost of smoke twirling in the air.

Sitting next to the candle and illuminated by the flame, a glistening glass of magenta-colored cabernet winked at her until she picked it up. Flicking the glass with her thumb and forefinger, she swirled the wine, then took a long deep sniff. She toasted to a glorious life with a beautiful, loving family and finally took a sip.

Leaning back, she allowed the early-evening air to caress her auburn hair, which spiraled to her bronzed shoulders. The ends turned a darker shade as they dipped into the water.

"*Ahh* . . ." Savannah repeated.

This was a good life. It was glorious to immerse oneself in the senses—hearing, smelling, and almost feeling the ocean waves break against the shore.

Savannah took another sip of the cabernet, enjoying the warm, smooth texture gliding down her throat. As the white organza curtain fluttered in the breeze and the late-day sun peeked in, she thought back to the first day she saw the seaside cottage she now called home. What an amazing six years it'd been. She sighed through a pensive smile and touched the glass to her open lips.

On the small table, candle smoke circled around smiling faces staring out at her from a picture in a weathered driftwood frame. It was her beautiful family. She held them in her warm hazel eyes, thinking how lucky she was and how much she loved them.

Savannah lost herself in the water and wine until she realized the sunlight had turned to dusk. She decided she'd better get out of the tub before she shriveled up like a prune. Lingering just one more moment, she gazed out the window as the sky invited the night, bringing with it thousands of twinkling stars and the majestic full moon. She tried to digest all the beauty surrounding her.

The sound of the tub draining the last of the bathwater woke her out of the dreamy state. Climbing out, she donned her nightgown and robe, then picked up a brush and ran it through her damp auburn curls. She smiled and hummed at the mirror.

Not too shabby for an almost thirty-six-year-old! she thought to herself. She was a bit on the short side of five-five and pretty trim now that she'd taken up running. Exchanging the brush for the empty wineglass, she tipped it toward the mirror as a toast to good health.

Heading downstairs, Savannah's mind wandered back to contemplate her most recent composition. In her distraction, she almost stepped on the curled-up dog at the foot of the steps.

She knelt down to scratch Jacey's ears. "You are such a special, good girl." She massaged the white fur curling around the dog's face. "I remember—as if it were yesterday—when I first met you and your very special friend. Wow. Where have those six years gone?"

Savannah looked over to notice there was a message on the phone. The caller ID showed that Mona had called while she was in the bath.

Oh boy, Savannah thought, shaking her head with a laugh. *I wonder what juicy news she has for me today! You can always count on Mona to be tuned in to what's happening in Abemly Shores!*

Savannah thought more about her dear friend as she began picking up the toys scattered around the living room floor. Mona was so funny, but she really did care about the people in their town. She was the first to show up with a house-warming gift of pastries, booties, and a list of babysitters for a new mom, or a sympathy basket for a family that needed help through hard times. She really was such a sweet and special lady.

Well, I guess that's why we chose her to be Lily's godmother, Savannah told herself.

Thinking of Lily, she couldn't believe their little girl would be three years old in July! And JJ—their wonderful, loving son—was finishing junior high and would soon be off to high school. It was amazing how time flies. She picked up one of JJ's Harry Potter books and set it on the sofa table, next to a photo of the dark-eyed, black-haired boy. He seemed to be looking right at her, showing the cutest dimple just to the left of his smile.

With the living room tidied up, Savannah headed next to the kitchen. Checking the fridge for leftovers, she found lasagna from dinner two nights before. It was just enough. She decided to whip up a quick salad while the lasagna was reheating. She turned on the oven, pulled out salad fixings, then turned back to the bottle of wine she had opened earlier for her bath.

One more glass on this lovely evening with dinner won't hurt! she thought. She poured it to let it breathe while working on the salad.

When dinner was ready, she put it on a tray and carried it out to the porch—with the dog at her feet—so she could enjoy the clear night air and fresh smell of the ocean. April was such an exciting month. There were new things to look forward to, and summer was in sight.

Once she finished dinner and the cabernet, she settled into a cozy chaise for a spell. A stack of books from Mona rested on the side table. Savannah picked one up—a romance novel. With a smile, she opened the book and dove in.

Startled, Savannah suddenly opened her eyes. At first she was confused, but then she sensed the familiar-scented breeze lingering on the porch. She smiled and stretched in the chaise.

As startled as Savannah, the curly white dog jumped up into Savannah's lap and snuggled in close to her. Savannah gave Jacey a loving hug and sighed as the scented breeze whipped around her, then took its leave.

"Oh, I must have dozed off . . . Everything's fine," she said to the night wind.

Satisfied that all was well, Jacey hopped down and returned to her spot on the floor.

Savannah found the romance novel still in her lap. As she turned to place it back on the side table, she noticed the old leather-bound history book from Mona's store. It had blown open—right to the page picturing the uninhabited land that now boasted the cottage.

With a shudder, Savannah stood up, gathered the remnants of her meal, and went into the house with Jacey at her heels.

Chapter 17

PERFORMANCE TOUR

April 14, 2012—Charleston, South Carolina

SAVANNAH GLANCED AT HER WATCH as she buckled her seat belt. It was 5:45 a.m. She was preparing for her flight to take off from Charleston.

Why do they even have flights this early? she thought. *The world should still be asleep, with everyone in bed!*

Then she smiled thinking of her family all tucked in at home. A tear escaped from her eye and dampened her cheek. It would be a long two weeks away on tour. Savannah reminded herself to just keep busy. Hopefully, she would be home before she knew it. And she could Skype with them every day.

Savannah took out a tissue to blow her nose, then she pulled out her music notebook. She began playing the notes in her head, clearly hearing her composition. Her blues piano had made such headway in the past few years. She was now known worldwide, and she had followers everywhere she went.

Honestly, it only made her home seem more appealing, welcoming, and safe. She actually couldn't wait till the day she could stop touring and stay in the town she loved. Savannah had cut her tours to one or at most two per year. She felt she owed it to her loyal fans. And actually, deep down, she enjoyed the love emanating from them when she performed. But being away from her family was harder and harder each time.

Someday, she thought, *I'll stop touring and just emit music to the world from lovely Abemly.*

Over the speaker, the pilot announced that the cabin doors were closed and that they were second in line for takeoff. Savannah popped a piece of gum in her mouth, straightened her music in her lap, and closed her eyes. In a few hours, she would arrive in LA to begin a whirlwind tour up the coast.

She couldn't help but think about the last time she had arrived in LA. It was quite a while ago, actually—about six months after the sudden storm that helped her discover her paradise town.

As the plane climbed to cruising altitude, Savannah decided to tuck her notebook away and pull out her iPad and headphones instead. She leaned her seat back and settled in for what she hoped would be a nice, relaxing nap. Complete with a down comforter and pillow, her oh-so-cozy first-class pod seat almost felt like her bed at home.

But as she closed her eyes, she continued to remember back to her last LA trip—when she had the disastrous evening with Mac, sliced his ear, and officially cut ties with him. The memories played over and over.

Seemingly seconds later, Savannah's eyes flew open when she felt a vicious jolt and heard tires squeal. The plane had touched down in Los Angeles. As she stretched her arms overhead, she sighed and chuckled a bit to herself.

Wow, I was really out of it. I must have been more exhausted than I thought. Sleeping coast to coast proves that these first-class pods are the only way to fly! Of course, nothing compares to being in my own bed, wrapped in the arms of my love.

Savannah quickly shook the thought away before homesickness really set in. She had to stop thinking about home, considering it was only day one of the fourteen-day tour. She had to stay strong and focused to get through this.

Just then, a flight attendant approached Savannah, asking if she would sign an autograph for an elderly couple who had recognized her as they boarded the plane.

"Yes, I'd be delighted to meet them and sign an autograph!" Savannah replied sincerely. As much as she preferred to be home rather than touring, she always appreciated her fans.

The attendant brought the couple up to meet Savannah, who then graciously offered to have a picture taken with them. The couple told her they were from a town not far from where she had grown up. They had heard her perform during her Hometown Tour the year before. The three of them chatted as they exited the plane.

Wishing them well, Savannah went ahead to baggage claim, where she caught a glimpse of a gentleman holding a sign with her hotel's name. She introduced herself and pointed out her luggage, which he quickly gathered up. He then escorted her to a waiting limo.

As they drove to the hotel, Savannah sipped her complimentary coffee, gazed dreamily out the window, and smiled. Her life had taken an amazingly better path compared to the last time she had come to Los Angeles.

After a good night's sleep, Savannah woke to a fresh breeze washing over her from the open window in her luxurious hotel suite. Listening, she heard a light rain gently tapping at the windowsill. There was just something so pure and cleansing about a spring rain. She sat up, pulled the blanket snug to her chin, and watched as the glistening drops found the window.

At that moment, her iPad alerted her to an incoming Skype call. Grabbing the tablet, she opened it to see her loving family blowing kisses and waving at her. Overwhelming warmth resonated from her toes to the top of her head as the happy faces greeted her.

"Hi, guys!" she said. "What's up?"

Much giggling came from the other party.

"This is your wake-up call!" JJ exclaimed.

"We miss you so much, Mommy!" Lily chimed in.

Jonas could barely fit his face in the screen as the kids hammed it up. Finally, he moved the screen a bit so Savannah could see him too.

"Hi, hon. We thought we'd have breakfast together and share what we're doing today, just as if you were home."

Savannah laughed. "That's a lovely thought, but we might have to wait a while if you want to share breakfast. I don't have—"

Just then, before she finished her thought, there was a knock on the door.

"Room service," a voice announced with another knock. "Room service. Or I can come back later if you aren't up, miss."

"Surprise!" JJ and Lily exclaimed.

Savannah grinned and blew a kiss to the faces on the tablet. They had called in room service to be delivered right at that moment. She threw on her robe and went to the door. Savannah pulled out her wallet, but the man at the door waved her off.

"No need, miss. It's already been taken care of!"

Savannah hurried back to the bed with her tray, ready to share breakfast with those she adored.

"Mmm! The food smells yummy!" she said. "Thank you, you guys!"

"We are having pancakes, sausage, and eggs—and so are you! Isn't this fun?" JJ said.

Lily giggled excitedly.

"The only difference is we have hot cocoa, and you have coffee," JJ continued. "And see? We even have a pink rose on the table, just like you have on your tray."

"This is a wonderful surprise! I miss you all so much already—and the tour is only beginning." Savannah turned from the screen to wipe a tear from her eye, trying not to let them see her cry. "You are the best—I love you so much!"

The family ate their breakfast and joked and talked about what was in store for each of them that day. Even though Savannah wanted to be with them all day, she knew she had lots to prepare for her performance that night. They decided they'd "meet" again in the morning for breakfast before she checked out of the hotel and headed north to the next tour location.

After ending their call, Savannah hummed happily, thinking of all the love waiting for her back home. In awe, she stepped into the enormous master bath.

What an amazing bathroom! she thought. *Too bad it has to be wasted on just one person. It would be a lovely—and roman- tic—experience to share with a certain tall, dark, and handsome man.* Smiling, she let out a soft purr under her breath.

There were heated marble floors and heated towel racks. A magnificent granite-topped vanity with mirrors seemed to go on forever.

There was also a state-of-the-art walk-in shower with more showerheads than she could count. It was surrounded by glass blocks lit internally, which took on an extremely romantic air. The glass appeared to be twinkling from within.

The pièce de résistance was the two-person Jacuzzi tub. A double step wrapped around the tub on three sides, and a huge glass-block window behind it let in light yet allowed for maximum privacy.

Savannah just stared in amazement, then let out a gentle sigh. *As incredible as that is, I still do love my cozy little tub at home. Nothing can take its place.*

With her rehearsal starting soon, Savannah opted for a shower. She slipped out of her plush hotel robe and hung it on the towel-heating rack so it'd be warm when she came out.

Stepping into the shower, she looked around, trying to figure out which faucets turned on which heads.

"Oh, what the heck," she said aloud. "Might as well live it up!"

Turning on the whole works, Savannah jumped and squealed when the pulsing water came at her from all directions!

She quickly adjusted all the heads at the proper height. At last, she sighed.

This is marvelous! I had no idea a shower could feel this good. Again, it's too bad my love isn't here to share it with me!

By the time she made it out of the shower, rehearsal would begin in an hour. Quickly, she dressed, clipped her hair up in a pony, and applied minimum makeup. She grabbed her music, purse, and sunglasses, then out the door she went to meet up with the limo.

The driver offered her another complimentary coffee for the ride to the concert hall.

"Actually," he said over his shoulder as he began driving, "my fiancée and I love your music. It's such an honor to meet you."

Savannah smiled. Once again, it was such a great feeling to connect with people who appreciated her music.

"Oh, thank you!" she replied. "You know what? I'd love to see if I can arrange for seats for you guys to this evening's concert."

Savannah and the driver chatted all the way to the concert hall, then he wished her farewell.

It was time for her to hit the keys, so to speak.

Chapter 18

A STRANGER IN TOWN

April 20, 2012—Abemly Shores

Sighing, Cassie pushed away from her desk, dropped the clean copy in her out-basket, and turned to her coworker Suz.

"Finally—it's Friday! I can't believe how this week never seemed to end. Do you have any plans for the weekend?"

"Not much going on," the young woman sitting at the desk across from her replied. "I think I'll catch up on my reading. I came across a great new book. Oh, and I've got an appointment at Viv's Cut 'n' Curl in hopes we can figure out how to tame this wild red mane of mine. Viv and I have been going back and forth for a while on this!" She tossed her long frizzy hair from side to side.

"Suz, your hair is gorgeous. I only wish mine had as much body as yours."

"Thanks, Cass," she said, laughing. "And since you're so enamored with my hair, I'll save you a lock for your locket! How about you—what are you up to this weekend?"

Cassie shrugged. "Nothing special. I thought about taking in the new chick flick at the theater, but I think I'll wait till next week, when Savannah is back so we can go together. I'll probably do some spring-cleaning at my apartment instead. That way, if there's a big lunch rush at the café, I'll be right upstairs so I can help out if the guys need me."

Glancing out the window toward the boulevard, Cassie suddenly caught a glimpse of a man carrying a small bouquet of flowers. He seemed to be coming toward the window, as if he knew them. That wasn't why he caught her eye, though. Rather, it was because of the way he carried the flowers—it was somewhat familiar. He held them down at his side and sort of upside down, swinging them slightly in time with his stride.

"Hey, Suz," Cassie said, turning back to her friend. "Do you happen to have a secret admirer you forgot to tell me about?"

"Yeah, right! What are you talking about, anyway?"

"That guy with flowers right—" Cassie looked back to point him out, but he was gone. "Hmm. Well, there was a guy right there, and it almost seemed as if he was coming over to the window to get your attention. Oh well. He's gone now."

"Dang," the redhead said with a smile. "And another one bites the dust!"

At that comment, Cassie just smirked and rolled her eyes. Then her other weekend plans suddenly came to mind.

"Oh, and I'm taking care of Lily for a while tomorrow so Jonas can get through the morning breakfast rush. I told Mona I'd come by Book Benders in the morning with Lily for a visit. We gals would love you to join us for coffee and pastries, if it works."

"Thanks! I just might need that break and some girl time after I lose World War XII with Viv. She always talks me into keeping my hair long. She tricks me every time because she has her magic 'wands' there in the salon, and she can tame my hair into something I never can. But then the next time, I'm mad because I can't re-create the magic!"

Chuckling, she shook her head so hard that her hair gave new meaning to "tame the wild beast." It totally looked as if it had a will of its own.

Cassie laughed and looked at her watch. "Well, that's it for me—another day, another dollar. Sylvie and I are meeting for a drink at the café. Why don't you join us? Come on, Suz—I think you need at least one to relax you before you face the big war tomorrow."

With that, Cassie threaded her arm through Suz's, steered her through the maze of desks, and led her out to the street. Once outside, they strolled on the brick walk toward the café, talking and laughing.

Suddenly, Suz let out a quiet squeal and squeezed Cassie's arm as she looked across the street. "Whoa! Did you see that guy? Now that's what I'm talkin' about!"

Cassie looked in that direction, only to catch a quick sight of well-worn cowboy boots meandering away. She took a few awkward steps as she tried to move forward and look back at the same time, craning her neck to see the man.

"Can you believe it?" Suz exclaimed. "It's raining men around here!"

Cassie laughed a little, but then she grew quiet.

As they entered the café, Cassie quickly spotted Sylvie in their favorite booth, the one tucked away in the corner. Sylvie waved toward the friends once she saw them too.

"Why don't you head over while I go say hi to Jonas?" Cassie suggested.

As she spun around, she almost bumped into JJ carrying a large tub for busing tables.

"Oh, hi there!" she greeted him. "It looks like you've got your work cut out for you tonight!"

A big grin came across his face. "Yep! It's really getting busy now. We sent Lily to Mona's so I can help Dad in the kitchen. Besides, Lily and Mona like to bake cookies together—and Mona always makes sure there are extras for Dad and me! She kinda likes to look after us when Mom's away."

"Is your dad in the kitchen? I'll just peek in and let him know I'm around if he needs more help."

Pushing open the door to the kitchen, Cassie caught Jonas in the middle of flipping a burger. When he turned to look at her, she laughed and held up her hands.

"Hey, don't let me stop a pro in action! I just want to pop in to offer a hand if you need one."

Jonas smiled, showing that great dimple of his. Cassie had always been content to call Jonas a friend, but she knew Savannah was one lucky woman to see that dimple all the time.

"Thanks, Cass, but I think my 'main man' and I have it covered for now. But it's good to know you're around. Are you heading upstairs for the night?"

"No. Actually, Sylvie, Suz, and I will be in the back booth having a drink. Maybe I can convince them to stay for dinner. What's the special tonight? It smells good!"

"Ham with my secret sauce, sweet potato, and your choice of veggies. It's pretty good, if I do say so myself." He grinned. "Hey, since we're a little backed up here, why don't you grab three glasses and a bottle of that nice pinot you like? It's on the house. I'll wait a bit, then send JJ out for your order. It'll make his day!"

"You're too good to me, but you've got a deal!"

"That's what friends are for!" he called out as she headed toward the door.

Cassie opened the bottle of wine and scooped up three glasses, then proceeded to the table where her friends waited, laughing and chattering away. When they saw the bottle, they both applauded her.

"Actually, it's your wonderful brother's treat, Sylvie—so thank him, not me. I should also mention that we will be dining here tonight as well. And there will be no excuses, or you'll be disappointing the waiter."

At that moment, JJ walked by, and she winked at him.

The friends ate, drank, and were merry—at least two of them were merry. As the evening went on, Cassie seemed to drift further and further away in her own thoughts. Finally, Sylvie spoke up.

"What's up with the faraway look? You barely touched your food. You better gobble it up, or Jonas will think you didn't like it!"

When Cassie barely managed a little laugh, Sylvie frowned. She reached out to touch her friend's hand.

"Really—are you okay, Cass? You just look like you're somewhere else tonight. Is something bothering you?"

"I know what it is," Suz chimed in. "You're wishing those hot cowboy boots were walkin' your way!"

"Honestly, Suz—sometimes I think you have a one-track mind," Cassie replied a bit sharply. "I didn't see that guy's face. You did. So maybe you're the one thinking about those boots—not me!"

Suz's face fell. "Sorry. I didn't mean anything. I was just making fun."

Before anyone could say a word, JJ was suddenly standing over them with a small pad of paper in his hand and a grin on his face.

"Ladies? If you are ready, I can take your dessert orders."

Sylvie smiled. "Well, my very handsome nephew, I would love a piece of the rhubarb pie. And what the heck—might as well make it à la mode. Anyone else joining me?"

Only Suz raised a hand.

"Cassie?" Sylvie asked, looking at her expectantly. "Are you sure you won't indulge?"

"I'm sure. Thanks, but I'm not feeling very well. Probably just tired. As a matter of fact, I think I'll pay and head on upstairs for the night. I have an early-morning date with Lily and Mona anyway. Good night—this was fun," she said, though her expression didn't seem to reflect the statement.

As Cassie left the table, Suz and Sylvie carefully exchanged worried glances.

"She was fine when we left work," Suz whispered. "But I'm telling you, seriously, she got pretty quiet after those cowboy boots went walkin'."

With a sigh, Cassie went upstairs to the apartment she rented from Jonas and Savannah. It was pretty well insulated, but when the café was really hopping downstairs, she could feel a little rumble through the floor.

She got into her pj's and slipped on a robe, then went into the kitchen to make some chamomile tea. She carried the teacup into the living room and plopped down on her favorite chair. Gently, she caressed the afghan her mother-in-law had made her so many years ago.

I don't know why I'm reminiscing about the Tanums, she thought. *I suppose I haven't spoken to them for a while. Maybe tomorrow I'll give them a call, just to check in and see how they're doing.*

Cassie remembered how devastated Charlie's parents had been when they heard he was gone. It just hurt too much to hang on to the ranch—with all its wonderful family memories. Instead, they moved into a little subdivision a few years back.

She picked up the album sitting on the coffee table and opened it to the first page. Carefully displayed was the paper she had written her first year in college, the one Charlie had thought he needed to help her with. A sad smile worked its way across her lips as she recalled the argument they'd had about it.

Well, she thought, *the paper made it into the newspaper even without his help.*

She turned page after page. The album was filled with articles that she and Charlie had written and had published at various times. They had used the album as a timeline for their careers, reviewing it often to better their writing in the future.

She chuckled to herself. *We were just a couple of geeks—but we were geeks in love.* A single tear dropped, dampening the page.

Downstairs at the café, Sylvie and Suz said good night to Jonas and JJ and walked out the door. Minutes later, a pair of boots walked in, topped off with a Stetson. The boots were attached to guy about six feet tall with unruly sandy-brown hair and green eyes that told stories of despair. A saddle-suede blazer hung loosely from one hand while the other hand gripped tightly around the neck of a well-loved guitar.

With a friendly smile, the cowboy walked up to the bar, where JJ was standing. "Looks like you're all set up for a singer, lil' pardner," he said, pointing to the small stage in the corner. "Who should I talk to about a singing gig?"

Just then, Jonas came out of the kitchen, tossing a dish towel over his shoulder. "Hi there," he greeted the cowboy. "Can I show you to a table? Or you can belly up to the bar, if that's your pleasure."

"Howdy. The name's Chuck," the cowboy said, reaching out to shake Jonas's hand. "I just got into town today. Ya see, I'm a journalist and doing some research around these parts. I also play this old guitar, and I have a pretty fair singin' voice. So, I was wondering if you were interested in hiring. I can work pretty cheap, since it's a second job."

"Well, Chuck, do you have a song in you right now—sort of like an audition?"

"Sure do," Chuck said.

Jonas gestured toward the stage area, so Chuck sauntered over, pulled up a chair, tossed his jacket over it, then sat down and began to strum. At first, he just hummed along with the tune. When he knew he had the diners' attention, he broke into song. The diners loved it, and some sang along. Even JJ stopped cleaning tables to listen and tap his foot to the beat.

When Chuck finished playing and the applause died down, Jonas went to talk to the stranger. "You were right— you are pretty good! Why don't you let me sleep on it? Stop by tomorrow afternoon, and we'll talk, Chuck."

"Sounds like a plan! And by the way, my friends just call me Slim. 'Slim Pickens.' Get it?" He took his hat off and slapped it across his knee. "I'll catch up with ya tomorrow. Thanks again, friend!"

Upstairs, Cassie had dozed off in her big chair, cuddled up with the afghan over her and the album in her lap. In her dream, she could almost hear Charlie singing and strumming his guitar.

She stirred, opening her eyes for a moment. *I'd almost forgotten about him playing guitar*, she thought to herself as the nice but peculiar dream faded away.

She decided to exchange the big chair for her even comfier bed. But first, she carried out her bedtime routine: she opened the drawer in her nightstand and took out the framed picture she kept there. They both looked so young—Cassie perched on that gentle horse while Charlie gazed at her, beaming with love. She smiled at it as memories flooded back.

I'll never forget, she thought.

As she returned the picture to the drawer, she grazed her fingers across the cherished small gold ring she also kept there. Then she drifted back to sleep.

It was 3:00 in the morning. Sweat dripped off Slim's toned, bronzed chest as he stumbled out of his hotel bed to the bathroom.

I need water, he thought. *My meds—where are my meds? This damn headache is like a vice tryin' to squeeze my brains out through my ears. Holy crap.*

He rubbed his eyes with the palms of his hands, trying to see the clock through his blurred vision. He was tired of waking up in the wee hours every night. It'd been happening more and more lately.

Man, will I ever sleep a full night again?

He sat in the chair next to the window with a glass of water and three pills. Vaguely, he remembered mumbling something. Yes, he had been mumbling in his sleep, and then he finally woke up in sweat. *What the hell was I saying?* But trying to remember only strained his mind even more.

He took the pills and chugged the water. He'd been dreaming too—as he did every night lately. *Aww, no way was I havin' that same dream again . . . All I remember is something about a horse and a baby—what the heck? Yea, I ride, but it's been a while. And the baby thing is way weird. I've never even been married, and to my knowledge, I've never fathered a kid!*

He leaned over and dragged his hands through his hair damp with sweat. He shook his head. *What is wrong with me? I've traveled the East Coast, seen scads of docs, but it's always the same: "Take these pills, and try to relax more. It'll just take time."*

In disgust, he threw the pill bottle across the room. It knocked over a tent advertisement sitting on the dresser. With a sigh, he slowly got to his feet to retrieve the bottle and put the advertisement back up.

The ad featured Viv's Cut 'n' Curl on one side and Jonas's Fine Café on the other. He glanced at the café ad. The photo was a poor facsimile, but he could still mostly make out the friendly faces of the employees. He recognized the young boy and the man he'd spoken to about the gig. But there was a blond woman . . . there was just something about her, with those big eyes.

Slim groaned in agony as a deep ache pulsed through his head. He bolted to the bathroom, vomited, then passed out.

Chapter 19

WHO'S WHO AT JONAS'S FINE CAFÉ

April 21, 2012—Abemly Shores

"DADDY, DADDY! WAKE UP! Time to have breakfast with my mommy yet?"

Dragging her cherished blanket behind her while still keeping a tight grip on the ear of her favorite stuffed dog, Lily climbed up onto her dad's bed. She jumped up and down, then bounced onto her knees, finally landing on top of Jonas. Her little blond curls tickled Jonas's nose while he still pretended to be asleep. Then she reached out her arms as wide as she could and gave him a hug.

"I love you, my daddy!" she said, planting a big sloppy kiss on his cheek.

Suddenly, Jonas rolled over with a silly roar. "You woke the lion, and now you must pay!" He began tickling his daughter until she was giggling so loudly that JJ and Jacey came bolting in to join the fun.

"Hey, Dad," JJ said, "how come you're still in bed? It's seven. Don't you have to open the café? Do you want me to ride my bike down there and start opening up?" JJ asked, hoping for a yes.

"No, but thanks anyway. Cassie is opening this morning since it's Saturday and she doesn't have to work at the paper. I also called in a new guy—Jack Grogan. He's going to help with busing and washing dishes. So, that means we can have a nice breakfast here before I have to go in to work."

Not being able to resist just one last tickle, he roared again and dove for Lily. She responded with shrieks of giggles. But then she sat up, trying to be serious.

"I miss my mommy. Call her now?"

"Lily, it's too early to call her right now," JJ spoke in his special big brother tone. "It's only four in the morning where she is. That's way too early to wake her."

"I have an idea," Jonas offered. "After JJ feeds Jacey, we can all go for a short walk on the beach. I'll even bring some of those blueberry muffins Mom made before she went on her trip. Lily, it's your job to brush your teeth and get dressed. And then right before we're ready to go, do you think you can remember to bring three bottles of chocolate milk?"

"Yes. I a big girl now. I going to play with Mona and Cassie today too."

Jonas gave her a hug. "Yes, you certainly are getting big—and very beautiful, just like Mommy! After our walk, it should be time for us to call Mom and have breakfast together."

"Are you going to tell Mom about that cool cowboy that might sing at the café?" JJ asked. "He was really good. And I guess you have to ask Mom if she's okay with it too."

"I liked him a lot too. I thought he was good and very charismatic with the audience. I think he'd be a good addition to the café. But you are very correct that Mom gets the last word on the hiring." Patting his son on the back, he added, "Now let's get this show on the road!"

Over at the café, Cassie flipped on the lights, then the music. She took one last look around to make sure the tables and chairs were in order and clean from last night. Using a stepladder to reach the chalkboard, she copied down the specials Jonas had jotted on a pad for her. Next, she went into the kitchen and started the grill, getting it warmed up for the morning rush. Over the years of helping Jonas at the café, she found she enjoyed cooking.

Humming to the music, she organized the prep area with everything she needed for omelets and the other breakfast food on the menu. Suddenly, she felt a presence. She was not alone. She spun around to come face-to-face with a paunchy man about five-foot-eight with a receding hairline. He was maybe in his late thirties to early forties. He didn't look terribly happy. He seemed to be staring at the ground, not looking her in the eye.

"Oh!" Cassie exclaimed. It took her a moment to collect herself. "You must be Jack. You scared me! Don't you know you shouldn't sneak up on people?" she said as she tapped his arm with a kind smile.

"Sorry," he mumbled.

"It's all right. Jonas mentioned you were coming in this morning. I'm Cassie. Happy to have the help. We should have a pretty productive morning."

When the phone rang, she glanced at the old clock on the wall and smiled. She knew who was calling.

"Good morning, Jonas," she answered.

"Wow! How'd you know it was me?"

"Lucky guess," she said with a smirk.

"How's it going?" he asked.

"Everything is *fine* here—and that's not a pun. I'm just working on the prep area now. I've got it all under control. I mean, *we* have it under control. Jack is here too." She glanced over her shoulder to make sure Jack was out of earshot. She lowered her voice anyway. "He scared me a bit when he came in, though. I was just glad I wasn't on the ladder at the time!"

Jonas let out a laugh. "Well, you can expect me in around nine thirty or so. The kids and I are going for a walk now. Oh, and Lily wants to make sure you don't forget your special date with Mona later this morning."

It was Cassie's turn to laugh. "I won't forget! Bye—have fun."

Just as Cassie picked up the large skillet, the phone rang again. She set it back down and reached back for the phone.

"Yes, Jonas, I'm still here," she answered. "I haven't left you high and dry just yet."

"How did you know it was me again?" he replied incredulously. "Am I really that predictable? Wait—don't answer that!" Jonas quickly got to the point. "I forgot to say that I'm thinking of hiring a musician. He stopped in last night for an audition—after you left, I think. He's really good. Did you hear him singing and playing his guitar?"

Cassie hesitated for a second. "No, I didn't hear any guitar music last night. I must have already fallen asleep. I think I dozed off in my chair. But he must be good if you're thinking of hiring him!"

"He said he'd come back today so I could give him my final decision. I told him to come in the afternoon, but just keep an eye out for him in case he drops in earlier."

"Well, if I see him, I'll just give him coffee and breakfast while he waits," Cassie replied.

At last, she was able to get back to the grill. She thought about this musician as she poured oil into the skillets to get them ready for the omelets.

Maybe I did hear a guitar while I was sleeping. But I thought it was just a dream. Who knows?

In a small room at Gulf's Inn just a few blocks off Main Street, Slim paced and stared out the window at the little stream below. Walking over to the mini fridge, he took out a bottle of water, then opened one of the pill bottles he'd strewn across the nightstand before he went to bed.

I've gotta get going on that article, but it sure is hard when those damn leprechauns won't quit their two-steppin' in my head. Maybe what I need is a strong cup of java to top off these pills.

Grabbing his keys and his Stetson, Slim took off for the stairs. He stopped in at the little restaurant in the lobby and ordered a coffee to go. He dropped a few dollars on the counter, tipped his hat to the waitress, and headed out.

As he opened the door to his truck, he hoped the hinges would hold. He heard the awful squeak and saw flakes of rust—which, once upon a time, had been green paint—float to the ground. Inside the cab, a folder lay on the passenger seat. The folder read, "Abemly Shores's Own: Forty-Year Anniversary of Vietnam Vet Remembered."

Slim gave a gentle good-luck tug on the bolo hanging on the rearview mirror, scooped up the folder, and closed the rusty door with yet another squawk. He walked around to the back of the old green truck and pulled down the tailgate with a thud. Setting his coffee and the paperwork off to the side, he hoisted himself up.

He gave his throbbing temples a brief massage before immersing his thoughts into the short life of a brave soldier. Slim jotted down notes as he read over the papers.

It was interesting—apparently this unfortunate soldier, Easton, left behind a girl. From what Slim could see, the couple had been pretty serious before he got called up. She never married. It wasn't hard for Slim to imagine that Easton had been the love of her life. She must have been devastated to lose him.

This woman was still living in Abemly Shores as the proprietor of a bookstore and coffeehouse. Taking a gulp of coffee, he decided he'd mosey down to Book Benders the next day for his morning java. Maybe he could work in a little interview with Ms. Mona Argyle.

But for now, he'd put the story on the back burner, so he could check out this little Southern town he found himself in. The people certainly seemed nice enough and trusting. *I mean, who hires a guy in this skin without asking for referrals?* he thought. *As I said—nice, trusting people. I just might want to stick around here for a while.*

As he walked, he spotted a building he had walked past the night before, only he hadn't realized how interesting and ornate it was. He read the plaque near the front door and saw that the building was home to the Abemly Shores newspaper.

"Wowzer," he said out loud.

What a fine piece of history the building was. Now there was a workplace for Slim. He wondered if they were hiring. He tried the door to no avail, then reminded himself that things often shut down on the weekend in these small towns. He made a plan to come back on Monday to introduce himself. He had written for other papers, but mostly in big cities. This could be the beginning of a whole new chapter for his résumé.

Continuing his walk up Main Street, he took in all the quaint shops and businesses. With each step, he became more enamored with the town. *Yes, sirree! This could be my new home.*

A redhead passed by on the boulevard. She gawked at him, then giggled when he tipped his hat to her and smiled.

Now he knew for certain he was home.

Jonas, JJ, Lily, and Jacey headed off for an early-morning walk on the beach. Lily was very intent on collecting the most beautiful shells she could find. Her plan was to string them all together in a necklace for her mom as a homecoming gift.

When they got back to the cottage, it was time to make breakfast, then call the hotel restaurant to try matching the meal for Savannah. Lily quickly ran outside and down the porch steps so she could pick flowers for the breakfast trays.

Once again, they enjoyed breakfast with Savannah via Skype. They laughed and shared stories about their days. Jonas told her about the singing cowboy. JJ chimed in about how great he was and how the customers really liked him.

"What do you think, Mom?" JJ asked. "Should we hire him?"

"Well," Savannah said, "considering your high recommendations, I agree that Slim sounds like a good addition to the café. I look forward to meeting him."

Everyone let out a little cheer and raised their glasses in a toast.

Soon it was time for everyone to say goodbye until the evening and get on with their days. They blew kisses to one another.

"Mommy," Lily said, "you have to come home in not too many days 'cuz I love you and miss you *soooo* much. And there's a secret—I making a surprise necklace for you!"

Chapter 20

THREE FOR TEA

April 21, 2012—Abemly Shores

CASSIE WAS CLEARING DISHES OFF A TABLE as Jonas walked into the café. She threw a glance at the clock.

"You're here nine thirty on the button!" she exclaimed.

He shrugged his broad shoulders and gave her one of his warm smiles. "As I said—I'm predictable!"

"How was your breakfast with the fam?" she asked. "How is Savannah doing out on the West Coast? I'm sure she's ready to come home—she must miss you guys so much!"

Jonas came over to help Cassie with the dishes. He picked up the empty coffeepot and a small pitcher of maple syrup. The syrup had oozed down the sides, making the pitcher stick a bit to the table.

"Yes, I think she's as ready as we are for the tour to be over!" He paused for a second, but Cassie's inviting eyes encouraged him to speak his mind. "Man, it just kills me when she's gone this long. I know she loves her music, and I know it's been such a part of her identity for most of her life. But I'll be happy when she doesn't do these long tours anymore! The kids miss her so much. You and Mona are wonderful, so don't get me wrong when I say this—but Lily needs her mom around. She's not even three yet. She's still a baby." He shook his head. "I guess I'm being selfish."

"Jonas, you are not being selfish. It's okay to love your wife and want your family together all the time. I don't blame you for thinking that way. Not one little bit."

Trying to conceal a sniffle, Cassie quickly turned to carry the dishes to the kitchen. But Jonas gently turned her toward him and took the dishes out of her hands.

"Cass, what is it? And don't try to tell me you just miss Savannah too." Bending his knees in order to get closer to her height, Jonas took her chin in his hand. "We've been friends for a long time. I know I can confide in you, and you know you can always confide in me."

"It's nothing. I'm fine. I must be getting a head cold. Or maybe it's the spring allergies attacking me." She sniffled again. "I better go check on that other table to see if they need more coffee."

Jonas smiled and shook his head. "I'll take care of the customers. You've been working the morning rush alone, so go take a break. Maybe you need something to eat. Besides, I believe you have a date with my daughter coming up soon, and we both know she will hold you to it!" A laugh spilled out of his mouth as he went back into the dining room.

Cassie headed for the bathroom to splash her face with water and blow her nose. She stared at herself in the mirror while she took the clip out of her hair. Her blond waves fell to her shoulders. But then her shoulders began to shake, and she hugged her arms around her stomach. She glanced up at the mirror again, only to see her big blue eyes filling with tears.

Jonas tried to understand. But nobody can know the pain that lives within me as I think about what could have been, the family I was supposed to have—my Charlie, our daughter.

It's been so long since Charlie's been gone. I just didn't want to believe he was really dead. I've daydreamed about him showing up at times, even made up different scenarios of how our reunion would be.

Cassie was so lost in a flood of emotions that she didn't even know how much time had passed before a knock on the bathroom door brought her to her senses.

"Cass, are you all right in there?" Jonas asked from outside. "Would you like to go upstairs and lie down?"

Cassie stared at herself once again. *This is stupid. Why do I let myself think about Charlie anymore? Honestly, it's been nine years! He's gone—it's over!*

After one last splash of cold water on her face, she was ready to open the door.

"Thanks again, Jonas, but I'm feeling better now. I suppose I should go get ready to pick up Lily."

"Are you sure? Otherwise, Mona will be just fine on her own."

"Oh no—I'd never stand up your adorable little daughter!" she said with a smile. "She'd never forgive me, and I definitely couldn't live with that!"

"I'm glad you feel better," Jonas said. "But what timing—that singer-slash-guitar player just stopped in while you were in here.

He seems like a nice, responsible guy. Real pleasant and personable. You know the type—somebody who gets along with everyone."

"I'm sorry I missed him!" Cassie said. "How did he ever come up with the idea of playing at the café? Is he from around here?"

"Well, I don't really know where he's from. He has a different drawl, sort of like the Western states. He goes by the name of Slim. He mentioned he's in town to do a story on one of our fallen Vietnam heroes."

A shiver ran down Cassie's spine. "So he's a writer. Interesting."

"Yeah, he said he's been traveling around, taking different assignments. He seems to be a drifter. I don't know how long he'll be in town, but he'll be a great addition while he's here."

Jonas eyed Cassie carefully and noticed her reaction about this man.

"Actually, if you want to stop in later this evening, he'll be doing a couple sets."

For whatever reason, Cassie had butterflies in her stomach. "Ah, yeah. I think I'd like that. Maybe I'll ask Suz to come with me. That is, if her appointment at Viv's is a success today. Well, I better get going. See you later."

"Okay. Have a great day. And don't let Lily be the boss of you!"

"That's impossible—she knows she already runs the show!" She laughed, giving his cap a tweak.

Watching Cassie walk out, Jonas wondered if maybe she'd be interested in Slim, the mysterious cowboy with a flair for writing and music. Even as he cooked and conversed with his customers all afternoon, he just couldn't get Cassie out of his mind.

I guess she's getting along okay. She has lots of friends—and all of us, of course. I only wish she could find someone special to finally get past Charlie. I wish she were as happy as Savannah and I are. But I just don't get it. It's like she's waiting for something.

Or someone.

Cassie drove under the canopy of trees that sheltered the path leading to the Beckman cottage. She suddenly thought about how Jonas had made his way up this same path years ago to see three-year-old JJ waiting for news about his mommy. It had to have been devastating! Everything changed for him and his family. But now the Beckman cottage—alias the Sills cottage—was filled with only happiness and lots and lots of love.

And speaking of love, Cassie's date was waiting patiently on the porch, all dressed up and carrying her purse. Behind her, JJ stood watch.

Cassie smiled. *My little sweetums—how adorable with all those blond curls blowing around in the wind, those bright eyes like her mom's, and that big dimpled smile she inherited directly from her dad! She is so beautiful. Who wouldn't want to just eat her up?*

But then Cassie had to fight back another sniffle as she put her hand to her heavy heart. What would her own daughter have been like?

Glancing toward the sky, she asked out loud, "Charlie, why did you leave me? We could have had a life together and maybe even other children. We were so good together. Why did you have to go?"

As she pulled up to the house, she grabbed a tissue to dry her eyes before getting out of the car.

"Cassie! I ready go!" Lily held her little arms out for a hug while being extra careful not to drop her fuzzy pink Minnie Mouse purse. "Lily will buy treat for you today!" She opened her purse to show Cassie the fortune she'd accumulated.

"Hi, sweetums," Cassie said, accepting the cuddly hug. "Oh, my—you do have a lot of money! But you'll have to make good choices as to how it's spent. I'm so excited for our special Saturday date! You look beautiful in your pretty sweater. Did JJ help you pick it out?"

"JJ help me, yes." She turned around to smile at JJ. "He my big brother. I love my JJ!"

"Well, we should get going now," Cassie said. "I bet Mona is getting hungry and wondering what is taking us so long."

Hand in hand, Cassie and Lily walked down the porch steps and skipped out to the car.

"Wait!" Lily held up her little hand like a police officer stopping traffic. She went to the flower garden and picked three pink roses. "For the treat party—me, you, and Mona!"

"You, little one, are truly a treasure!" Cassie gave her a kiss as she helped her into the car seat.

Once they arrived at Book Benders, Cassie parked the car and helped Lily out of her seat. As soon as those little pink shoes touched the ground, Lily ran into the waiting arms of her godmother. She immediately stuck out a hand that tightly held a pink flower.

"I pick flower for my Mona. We love pink, right?" With such a deliberate nod of her head, those curls once again went into motion. "Where Josie?"

"Hello, my little love. Josie is in the shop waiting to see you." Mona winked at Cassie as they followed Lily inside.

"She really is something, isn't she?" Cassie said.

"She sure is!" Mona agreed. "Is there any word from Savannah? I'm sure she misses this little princess a lot!"

"She seems good, but I'm sure she misses everyone. And I know Jonas is more than ready to have her home!"

"Wheee!" Lily squealed as she saw Josie. She always hugged Josie—whether Josie wanted a hug or not. "She Jacey's mommy. Jacey miss her too!"

She then went up to Mona with a dollar in her hand. "For cupcake and hot chocolate," she explained.

Mona thanked her immensely for the money, then placed it in a piggy bank she kept for Lily's college fund.

"This for Cassie," Lily said, handing her two shiny quarters.

Keeping a straight face as much as she could, Cassie also deposited the coins in the pink piggy bank.

They all sat down at the table near the antique books. Mona picked out a book about a boy who wanted to play piano, and she and Cassie took turns reading it to Lily. Then Lily attempted to read it back to them.

"My mommy play piano," Lily informed them. "I do piano trips when I grow up too."

"Lily, honey," Mona said, "why don't you go pick out a new book to take home?"

As Lily ran to search the shelves designated for children's books, Mona and Cassie sat chatting.

Soon, they heard giggling coming from the children's area, so they went to see what Lily found so amusing. She had a book in her hand. On the cover was a cowboy riding a horse and waving his hat in the air. Lily pointed at the window and giggled again.

"Man with hat say hi to me! Man like me. He laugh!"

Chapter 21

TWO HEADACHES CLOSER
TO AN ANSWER

April 21, 2012—Abemly Shores

SLIM SAT ON A BENCH LOOKING OUT over Abemly Sound. The sun was beginning to set as the world began to turn a fiery shade of crimson around him. Nursing yet another blasting headache, Slim listened to the waves gently rolling in hopes it would calm his head.

> *Maybe it's time to check out some holistic doctors. I'd even try acupuncture at this point. When I suggest an X-ray or CT scan, they tell me I'm overreacting and that it would be an unnecessary exposure to radiation. Well, then, I'd like them to explain away this damn intense pain!*

Holding the guitar in his lap, he began to strum. He played the chords, then hummed along and picked, creating the tune as he went. A playful breeze kicked up, causing the marsh grasses to bend and sway. In response, the water took on an easy ripple effect. Slim closed his eyes as the breeze tiptoed over his eyelids in a soothing, hypnotizing trance.

The tune he played seemed to be coming directly from his heart. It was mellow, soft, and somewhat reminiscent of another time and place. Thinking he'd heard it before or maybe even written it some time ago, he felt totally comforted by the familiar melody.

He felt a light numbing around his temples as the pain lifted to a submissive state. Slowly, he opened one eye at a time to make sure the pain wasn't waiting to pounce unexpectedly, like a cheetah after its prey. Feeling extremely relaxed for a change, he took a deep breath, then exhaled. Still no pain.

Checking his watch, he got to his feet, still holding on to that special guitar. He started meandering toward Jonas's Fine Café while still humming the tune that had originated deep in his soul.

Seeing a familiar name pop up on caller ID, Cassie picked up her cell phone from her nightstand. "Oh, hi there, Suz. How did your hair turn out?"

"Fabulous. It's still long but perfect—today anyway. I wasn't certain I liked it until I was walking up the street and I saw that long drink-a-water with awesome boots and a body to match. He tipped his gorgeous Stetson to me and smiled. Oh gosh—I thought I'd just melt there on the spot! So I figure if my hair was good enough to catch his eye, well, then, it's good enough!"

"So, am I to assume we're heading over to the café tonight to listen to the cowboy play? Hmm?"

"Duh!" Suz said with a laugh. "Should I come over to your apartment first?"

"Sure, that sounds good. And what about having a bite to eat too? Jonas makes the best burgers in town, you know."

"Well, you are a bit biased now that you work there!" Suz fired back. "I'm excited. What time should I be there?"

"How about seven? I don't think Slim is due to start until eight, so that'll give us time to have a drink and order food before it gets too busy." Cassie paused for a moment, hesitating. "And Suz, don't think you have to get all gussied up for tonight. I know you say this cowboy is dreamy, but we're just hanging out at the café, remember?"

"Yeah, yeah, I get your drift. Besides, when he gets one look at you, I'll be yesterday's potatoes."

Cassie couldn't help but break out into hysterical laughter. "You are just too funny for words! See you at seven, then."

Cassie hung up, still laughing. But then she realized it was now just nervous laughter. Her stomach fluttered, and she felt a little shaky.

I have no idea why I'm nervous. We're only going to the café to listen to music and grab a burger. But wow, am I a mess! You'd think this was a first date or something.

As Cassie stewed over her thoughts, she absentmindedly slid open the nightstand drawer and ran her hand over the photograph. After a moment, she jumped to her feet and stared into her closet, letting out a sigh.

I don't know what to wear. But what does it matter, anyway? My gosh, I'm just going downstairs to meet Suz. I could wear my pj's! I don't think anyone really cares.

Perhaps ignoring her own thoughts, Cassie reached for her denim skirt. *Well, what could it hurt to throw on a jean skirt? That's still pretty casual.*

Now she needed her low heels to complete the look. Kneeling, she began to dig through the closet. *How could I have lost those shoes? I wore them just last week. And this closet isn't exactly something out of* Rich and Famous!

Crawling in farther and reaching to the back, she knocked something over.

"What in the world?" she said aloud.

She pulled a pair of camel suede boots out from under the mass of clothing. She sat down on the floor, holding one of the boots in her arms. She traced the blue-and-pink-stitched design with her finger. As she touched the soft leather, a memory hit her square in the eyes.

I remember when Charlie and I bought these. It was right before he took me to meet his parents at the ranch. He said, "Little Darlin', you should have a good pair of cowgirl boots so you can legitimately cross the border into Texan country!" I didn't even know I still had these. I can't believe I'd kept them after all these years!

She brushed dust off the other boot as she tried to hold back the sobs building in her chest. *Oh, he was something, that husband of mine.*

Forcing herself to her feet, she slipped into the skirt, added a lightweight sweater, and pulled on the old boots. *Yes, I think these will be perfect with my jean skirt. I may as well get some use out of these boots, since I found them tonight for whatever reason.*

She grinned when she stopped to look at herself in the full-length mirror behind the bedroom door. *It is kind of fun to dress up a bit, I guess. If nothing else, Suz will get a kick out of it.*

Cassie headed next to the bathroom to do her makeup. It wasn't long before she heard footsteps running up the outside stairs to the apartment just before she heard a knock on the door and a female voice singing a country song.

"Come on in, Suz," Cassie called out. "I'm just finishing my makeup."

Suz let herself in. She laughed as she came around the corner to peek in the bathroom.

"A skirt? Oh sure! See? Even though you said not to get 'gussied up,' I knew you'd try to make a good impression on the cowboy. Now I don't have a chance in a million—"

Suddenly, Suz stopped midsentence as her eyes fell to Cassie's boots.

"Wow! What's with the boots? They are way cute! Now he'll fall in love at first sight! He'll think you're one of his kind. You know—Western boots and a jean skirt. It looks like you're headin' off to a rodeo or ranch or something. Are you gonna put a hat on too?"

To Suz's surprise, Cassie plopped down on the side of the tub and buried her face in her hands. "You don't like it! I knew it—it's a stupid look! And I promise—I am not trying to egg this guy on! I was actually just digging in the closet for my low heels and found these boots way in the back. It just seemed to work since I was wearing this skirt anyway."

"Cass, I'm just teasing you," Suz reassured her. "You really do look great. And no, I don't think you're trying to 'egg him on'—even though with one look at you he'll be knocked over with a feather."

Cassie chuckled a bit. "Well, you look just as good. You'll draw plenty of attention with that adorable dress and your gorgeous hair! I do love how Viv did it with the cascading curls and the barrette pulled to the side. It's a great look for you."

Suz smiled. "Thanks, girlfriend! Well, we better get downstairs so we can get a good seat close to the stage." She gave Cassie a wink and a dreamy look, then burst out laughing. "Oh, you know I'm only kidding around! If I didn't kid, I wouldn't be me! But seriously, though, let's get that corner booth near the stage. That's the best spot in the house!"

The women headed downstairs to the café. Once situated in the corner booth, they tried to decide on a bottle of wine.

"Should we stick with the merlot, or change it up a bit?" Suz asked. "Maybe we could get Jonas over here for some recommendations."

Cassie glanced over at Jonas practically flying from table to table. "Tell you what," she said. "I'll head back to the bar and see what bottles we have in stock. It's getting pretty busy, and Jonas looks a bit overwhelmed. Let's not bug him. You stay here and take a look at the menu. When I come back, I'll put in our food order so Jonas won't have to worry about us at all."

Rather than head to the bar, though, Cassie made a detour to the kitchen to check on Jonas. Just then, Slim walked through the front door. He headed to the stage to begin setting up.

Suz just couldn't sit still and watch. She had to go over and introduce herself.

"Hi there," she greeted him. "My name is Suzanne, but you can call me Suz." She grinned sweetly ear to ear. "I hear this is your opening night at Jonas's Fine Café. We're all really excited. We think of our little Abemly Shores as a musical town. I'm sure you know that Jonas's wife, Savannah, is a jazz pianist and composer. She'd be here tonight if she weren't on her big West Coast tour."

"Nice to meet you, Suz," Slim said, tipping that magnificent Stetson once again. "My name is Chuck, but friends call me Slim. I hope I can make myself proud entertaining you and your friends here in Abemly. I sure am enjoying your town. Well, I better be gettin' back to what I was doin'," he said, tipping his hat again and giving her a wink.

"Oh, hey—I just have one question," Suz said, not quite ready to mosey on back to the booth. "I think I saw you on the boulevard yesterday. You were carrying flowers. So, I was wondering, who were they for?" She eyed him expectantly, silently praying they weren't for a girlfriend or something.

"My, you are the inquisitive type, aren't you?" Slim was a bit annoyed, but then he let out a pleasant chuckle. "Actually, I'm a writer here on an assignment for an article about Easton Baines, the war hero. I felt that the honorable thing to do was introduce myself to him at his grave site, so I brought flowers. Just somethin' I like to do when I write an article about the deceased. Anything else you'd like to know, Suz?"

"No, nothing else," she answered with a giggle. "Sorry I took up so much of your time. I talk a lot—as you probably noticed. Well, I'll just get back to the booth over there, where my friend and I will be sitting." Smiling, she turned to head back to the booth, but then she stopped and spun around. "Oh, and I think that's very thoughtful of you to take flowers to Easton's grave!"

Slim shook his head with a smile. Taking the stage, he sat down to tune the strings and do a quick warm-up. He hummed along and sang a few words as he played.

From the corner booth, Suz watched his every movement with stars in her eyes.

Back in the kitchen, Cassie couldn't help but jump in to cut some veggies for the salads and burgers. From over at the grill, Jonas gave her an appreciative smile.

"Thanks, Cass. You're a lifesaver. This is a pretty special night with Slim playing, and I hate to get too backed up. I don't want you to miss the show, though. I mean, it's not even your night to work. Jack was supposed to come in, but he called to say there was some sort of situation with his wife—he had to stay home. He seemed pretty upset."

"No problem," Cassie replied. "I'm happy to help. Besides, I'm sure Suz isn't missing me for a minute. She's probably ogling that singer of yours." She paused for a second. "Hey—he must be starting. I hear his guitar."

Cassie listened carefully as Slim crooned the first few words of an original song. As if in a trance, she suddenly dropped her knife, sending it clattering to the floor.

"Is everything all right over there?" Jonas asked, glancing in her direction. "It's not like you to have the dropsies."

Cassie shook her head to clear it. She bent down to pick up the knife and put it in the sink, then she washed her hands before grabbing a new one.

"I'm fine—I guess it just slipped," she said, still somewhat confused. She quickly finished up the veggies. "Is there anything else you need?"

"No, but thanks. Make sure you grab a nice bottle of wine for you and Suz. It's on the house—my thank-you for helping tonight. Also let me know what you want for dinner, and I'll get it out to you."

"Sounds good! I'll go check with Suz, then I'll be right back with our order."

Cassie headed back to the corner booth, where Suz sat looking at the menu. When Suz noticed Cassie approaching, a smirk crept across her face.

"Oh, how nice of you to join me! Are you going to sit down now, or do you plan to run back and forth to work in the kitchen all night?"

"Hey, don't get bossy with me! Remember, I know where you live!" Cassie said with a laugh. "Honestly, though, I'm sorry I got held up in the kitchen. It's just that Jonas is so busy—I feel guilty not working tonight!"

Then Cassie looked toward the stage, suddenly realizing there was no music.

"Hey, where's Slim? I thought he had started his set."

"Oh, he was just warming up. I think he's taking a quick break now, before he actually starts. He'll be back soon."

Cassie felt butterflies in her stomach for some reason. Once again, she shook her head. Changing the subject, she pointed to the menu.

"So, have you decided what you want so I can get the order to Jonas ASAP? And what wine would you like? Because I helped out in the kitchen, he said it's on the house. You're welcome, by the way. It's nice having me for a friend, isn't it?"

"Yeah, yeah. I'm so lucky." Suz rolled her eyes, then studied the menu one more time. "How about Café Burgers with cheese curds and the house red?"

"Got it," Cassie replied. "I'll be right back—I promise."

Cassie disappeared into the kitchen; seconds later, Slim sauntered out of the restroom. Heading to the stage, he picked up the guitar and placed the strap over his shoulder. He planned to open with an original, the one he had sung while sitting on the bench and feeling the breeze kindly wash away his pain. But first, he had to introduce himself. With the pick between his fingers, he strummed once to get the patrons' attention.

"Howdy there, friends! I can't tell you how honored I am to be able to share my tunes with y'all tonight. And a big thanks to Jonas and his family for inviting me to play in this 'fine' establishment, no pun intended," he said with a chuckle. He tipped the mighty Stetson with that special quirky smile of his. Beginning to strum the guitar and tap his foot, he spoke in a singsong voice, "Just call me Slim. And I do believe it's time to get this show started!"

After placing the food order with Jonas, Cassie went behind the bar to get two glasses and pop the cork on a house red. With one hand, she picked up the glasses by the stems. With the other, she grabbed the newly opened bottle.

Just as she came out from behind the bar, Slim broke into song. Instantly, Cassie's stomach flip-flopped.

And then the wine, the glasses, and—last but not least—Cassie crashed to the floor.

Even over the music, the shatter and thud was loud enough to make everyone jump and spin toward the sound. Suddenly, the music stopped. Everyone gaped at the woman down on the floor with glass all over her and red wine pooling at her feet.

Jonas happened to be at a nearby table, taking an order from Mona and Cecilia and John Sills. Like a well-oiled emergency-response team, Jonas raced to the kitchen to retrieve some smelling salts, Mona rushed to Cassie's side, and Cecilia grabbed her phone to dial 911.

Mona was relieved to see that Cassie was semiconscious.

"It can't be you . . ." Cassie mumbled. "Why? Where?"

Jonas returned, kneeling down to waft the smelling salts under Cassie's nose. With him at Cassie's side, Mona next went behind the bar to wrap ice cubes in a cloth to put on Cassie's forehead.

As all this took place, Suz slowly but surely pulled her attention from Slim, saw what had happened, and finally raced to her friend's side.

"Cass!" Suz exclaimed in her own frantic manner. "Are you okay? Do you need an ambulance? Man, you don't look so good!"

Cassie slowly opened her eyes and managed a weak smile. "Thanks, Suz. I can always count on you when I'm down and out!"

Putting down his guitar, Slim hurried over to Cassie and began fanning her with his hat. When she turned toward him, he smiled.

"Hey, there you are, Little Darlin'. How ya doin'? You surely do have everybody hoverin' over you."

"How? Where?" was all she could get out.

Then she fainted again.

Once the paramedics arrived, they stabilized Cassie and checked her over. Determining she didn't need additional medical attention, they helped her get comfortable upstairs in her apartment. Suz announced she would stay overnight to keep an eye on Cassie.

With Cassie settled in her bed, Suz brought her some chamomile tea. She sat next to her while Cassie slowly drank most of it.

"What in the world happened?" Suz gently asked as Cassie handed back the teacup, clearly ready to rest. "You gave us all a scare. I'm so glad you weren't seriously hurt."

Cassie reached out to squeeze her friend's hand as her eyes began to close.

Suz smiled tenderly down at her. "Well, Slim says he hopes you'll feel better soon."

Hearing Slim's name again, Cassie frowned with her eyes still closed. She started to mumble again.

"How? How could this be?"

Suz headed to the couch as her friend drifted off to sleep in the next room. Pulling a blanket over herself, Suz wondered what had caused such a reaction in Cassie.

Why did she faint when she came out and saw Slim playing? I mean, yeah—he's really hot. I'll agree to that! But it's not like Cassie to get that excited about a guy. And then why did she faint again when he came over and called her Little Darlin'? I thought that was really sweet!

Chapter 22
THE STORM

April 22, 2012—Abemly Shores

IN THE WEE HOURS OF THE MORNING, a loud, thunderous crash of lightning bolted across the sky, accompanied by clouds spewing torrents of rain. Cassie thrashed and whimpered uncontrollably in her bed, blurting out names from her past.

Without warning, the roaring wind broke through her bedroom window with a smashing of glass. It was followed by the uninvited rain dousing the sill and floor below. The ferocious wind swept through the room, as if searching for some hidden treasure. Closet doors and dresser drawers flew open. Yet still Cassie slept.

With one last brazen attempt, the determined wind knocked over the nightstand. It caused the drawer to fall out, which in turn exposed a photo. Confident she'd completed her task, the wind shot out the window as abruptly as she'd entered it.

Hearing all the commotion, Suz fell off the couch, scrambling to reach her friend's bedroom as quickly as possible. In her frantic rush, she tipped over a lamp and sent it crashing to the floor.

Finally running into Cassie's room, Suz yelled, "Holy crap! What is going on in here?"

The bursts of lightning outside illuminated the room enough for Suz to see that Cassie was somehow still sleeping.

"This storm could wake the dead!" Suz exclaimed. "How can you be sleeping? Cassie, wake up!"

Suz flipped on the light switch and surveyed the damage. There was glass everywhere, and the rain was still driving in through the window.

"Oh my God—the wind was so strong it broke your window. What a mess! Cassie, you've got to wake up!" she said, now shaking her friend. "You're scaring me!"

At last, Cassie stirred enough to open her eyes. "What is it?" she asked groggily. Then she let out a groan. "Oh, my head is killing me. I'm so dizzy . . ."

And like that, she closed her eyes again and drifted back to sleep. Instantly, Cassie dreamed of a young blond woman spinning around her room, opening doors and drawers. Then the woman tiptoed toward Cassie with a photo in her hand and a smile on her face.

In the meantime, Suz looked for something to put over the broken window. At last, she spotted a poster backed by cardboard. It was an image of Clint Eastwood in *The Good, the Bad and the Ugly*. Suz remembered when Cassie had purchased it at a consignment shop.

"Sorry, Clint!" she said as she separated the picture from its backing. She then pressed the cardboard into the window frame in hopes of holding off the rain until someone could find a more permanent solution.

Next, she picked up as much of the glass as she could. Then she scurried about the room, trying to clean up. She closed all the doors and drawers that had somehow flown open.

When she picked up the nightstand and slid the drawer back in place, she found a picture frame facedown on the floor. An envelope was taped to the back. Fearing the glass had shattered in the crash, Suz turned the frame over. Miraculously, it was in one piece.

Suz paused when she noticed the photo. It was obviously Cassie, several years younger. She was sitting on a horse.

Hey, those are the same boots she wore earlier, Suz thought.

Now Suz looked more closely at the picture. Cassie was holding one foot out, as if showing the boot off to the camera. She looked so happy. There was a man standing next to the horse with his arm around it and stroking its head. The man had a warm smirk and leaned his head toward Cassie.

What a great picture. But I wonder—is that her husband? Weird that I've never seen a picture of him before.

Suz stared at the man in the photo. *If I didn't know better, I'd think that our cowboy, Slim, is this guy's older brother.* Shock came over Suz as she took another look. *It can't be! But what if?*

So many questions flooded Suz now. Was it really possible that Cassie's "dead" husband wasn't dead at all? But then where had he been all those years? Did Cassie recognize him last night in the café? Was that why she passed out? But shouldn't Slim have recognized her too?

Suz glanced at the clock, which was blinking 3:10 from a short power outage. She shook her head.

No. I must be crazy. That must not be Slim in the picture. This whole weird storm just has me hallucinating, that's all!

Cassie was still sleeping, her face pulled tight in a frown. Suz decided the best thing to do was to make some chamomile tea—with maybe some schnapps on the side—then go back to bed out on the couch. She put the picture upright on the night-stand and headed to the kitchen.

But right before she turned the burner on the kettle, Suz remembered she had left the light on in Cassie's room. When Suz returned to the room, she was startled to find Cassie sitting up in bed, staring at the photo.

"Cass!" Suz exclaimed, surprised to see her friend awake. But then she saw the tears streaming down Cassie's face.

"Oh my God, Cass. It's really true, isn't it? It's him—your Charlie."

Cassie could barely find the words to speak. "I . . . I . . . I don't know why he didn't recognize me. He looked right at me, even called me Little Darlin'. But he didn't seem to know me from Adam! It was as if our life together had just been some figment of my imagination." She began to sob again. "I can't imagine where he's been for nine years or why he left! He never would have pretended to be dead. He never would have run away from our marriage."

Suz frowned. She hated seeing her friend's pain and confusion.

"Well, let's think about this logically. Are you sure it's him?" she ventured. "You said it's been nine years since you saw him. Maybe Slim just looks a lot like him. I can understand how that would still cause a reaction for you."

Cassie's sobbing eased a bit as she gave this some thought. "Maybe you're right. But if it isn't him, then oh wow, does this guy really look and sound like him! I mean, my Charlie was a singer-songwriter and played guitar too, just like Slim."

"He's still in town, so I'm sure you can get this straightened out. Maybe you can meet him for coffee soon—then you'll really know it's him. Maybe he didn't get a good enough look at you tonight when you fainted. Maybe he'll recognize you this time." Suz smiled. "Look at it this way—if it's really him, then you get your husband back and you get some answers about what happened all these years. If it isn't him . . . well, then you're simply back to where you were before you saw Slim."

"Oh, Suz—if only it were that easy. You do have a point, though. I'll meet him for coffee, and we'll talk. I'm sure I'll figure it all out." Then she grimaced and squeezed her eyes shut. "This is just too much. Oh, my aching head!"

"Okay, Cass—we should get some rest. You know what they say: things always look brighter in the morning."

Cassie nodded and settled herself back in bed. Suz turned off the light, then headed for the kitchen. It was time for that schnapps.

After tossing and turning in his hotel room bed, Slim got up and walked to the window, which had blown open in the storm. Rain was trickling down the wall. Slim closed the window, then froze, holding his head.

Oh man. There's that damn pain again. Where are my pills?

He made it to the mini fridge to grab a bottle of water. He popped three pills, guzzled down the water, then stared out at the occasional light show in the night sky.

Slim thought about what a strange night it had been with that poor woman fainting during his first set. He felt so bad about her. He didn't even know her name.

Still . . . there was just something about her in that split second when she opened her big blue eyes before she fainted again. She did have amazing blue eyes. Something about them was mesmerizing. It gave Slim an odd feeling, almost an all's-right-with-the-world feeling.

Slim decided he'd stop by the café later to see how she was doing. He could at least introduce himself and apologize if he had scared her.

He picked up his guitar and lightly picked at the strings for a second. He had a hankerin' to play. But it was the middle of the night. He didn't want to wake the other people in the inn.

The ache in his head throbbed again. He crawled back into the bed, laying the guitar beside him.

Damn little people doin' that two-step in my head. Would you pipe down so I can get some rest? Pretty please?

He closed his eyes and found himself instantly thinking about that woman from the café again.

Flowers—yes. I'll bring flowers when I pay a visit to Little Darlin'. Strange. Why did I call her Little Darlin'? That's just not something I'd say to a woman.

But those are the most amazing blue eyes I've ever seen. There's just something familiar about them.

He pulled his guitar into his hands. Quietly, he strummed and sang "Blue Eyes of Abemly" until he fell asleep.

In a small bungalow, Jack Grogan also awoke from the storm. For a few minutes, he watched his wife, Cheylene, finally enjoy a peaceful moment of sleep, thanks to the meds the doctor gave her. Finally, he got out of bed and paced the room.

He didn't know how much longer he could stand watching his Chey in such pain. After being laid off from his job as foreman on a construction site that went south, he had been forced to take on three part-time jobs. The newest one was at the café.

All we have is this tiny piece-of-crap two-bedroom house, he thought. *Yet I still can't pay the bills. The bank is talking about foreclosing. I just don't know what I can do anymore.*

He walked to the bed and gently rubbed his wife's arm as she slept.

And now we've lost another babe. Dammit! I know I'm no good. But why is Chey being punished? She's a good woman. She works real hard to give us a good and happy life. I'd go to the moon to give her what she wants. All she wants is a baby. But every time she gets pregnant, it's taken away from us. Why?

Last year, she miscarried shortly after the first trimester. And last time, she had to quit her job at the grocery store because the doctor said she was high risk. But after all that, she lost the baby anyway. It pushed her over the edge!

And now we can't even get a baby through adoption either. We turned in the damn application months ago but have heard nothing. Probably all my fault 'cuz I'm a no-good bum.

A loud crack of lightning made Chey stir. "Jack?" she asked, realizing he wasn't lying next to her. "What's going on?

Sounds like it's stormin' bad out there. Why don't you come back to bed and get warm under the quilt? I'll give you one of those neck rubs you like. Maybe you can relax and get some sleep."

"Hush now. Don't you fret about me, hon. I'm fine. I'll be right back. I'll go get us somethin' warm to drink to take the chill off. You just keep warm and rest," he said. He tucked the bedding around her and kissed her cheek.

Jack went to the kitchen. As he mixed up some hot chocolate, he thought about being in the park the other day—how happy those families seemed to be. In his head he confirmed, *We will be a family just like them, with little children runnin' round, giving their mom big hugs and kisses. Yeah, Chey, you're gonna have the family you deserve!*

When he took the hot chocolate back to the bedroom, he found his wife sound asleep again. So he set the drink on the nightstand, crawled into bed next to her, and delicately gathered her in his arms. It was as if he were holding a fragile, priceless, cherished piece of art. He fell asleep dreaming of his Chey and the child they would soon share.

Under a beautiful pink-flowered canopy covering a four-poster bed, a little girl cried as she hid under her covers, her blond curls all askew. Thunder crashed and unforgiving rain beat on the window as if trying desperately to get in. Trying to get her—just like the bad people in her dream. They were trying to get her too.

Lily peeked out from under the safety of her covers just as lightning shot through the sky. A shadow from a tree resembled a crooked old witch flying toward her! She screamed. When the sky lit up in force, she screamed again, but this time jumped out of bed. As she flung open her bedroom door and rushed into the hall, she ran right into the arms of her big brother, JJ.

"Help! Help! Her is after me!" She jumped onto JJ, wrapping her arms and legs around him so she was no longer touching the floor. "JJ, don't let bad people get me! I scared! I want my daddy!"

"Lily, it's okay. I have you now. No one can hurt you. I'm your big brother, and I'll always keep you safe."

Jonas was now out of bed and out in the hall too. Lily jumped out of JJ's arms and ran to him.

"Daddy, Daddy! My JJ save me from big monster! I scared, but JJ scare monster away. Him help me." She grabbed Jonas's leg and wouldn't let go. "Me sleep in your bed, Daddy. It okay, yes?"

"Of course, little Lily," Jonas said, picking her up and holding her protectively in his arms.

"Me have bad dream, Daddy. Bad people want to take me away." Big tears started dripping from her big hazel eyes. "Me don't want to go away, Daddy! Please don't let them take me. Me want to stay at my house!" Her cries turned into sobs. She even began kicking her feet. "Pleeeaase, Daddy!" she pleaded.

Jonas and JJ exchanged looks of concern.

"Oh, my sweet baby," Jonas said soothingly. "That must have been some nasty nightmare. But you're safe now. Everything is fine. We all love you very much, and we'll always be together!" He hugged her tightly, swaying while patting her back gently. "Mommy, Daddy, and JJ love you so much!"

"Jacey too?" Lily asked, trying to catch her breath. She bobbed her head up and down, causing her curls to bounce. "And my Mona and Cassie?"

"Yes, sweetie. Jacey, Mona, and Cassie love you too. And all your grandparents, aunts, uncles, and cousins," Jonas reassured her.

"Man with hat—he like me?" she asked with a smile, now a bit giddy through her tears.

Unsure, Jonas looked at JJ, who just shrugged.

"Well, I'm not sure who the man with the hat is," Jonas said. "But I'm sure he likes you too. Now, let's go get some sleep. Before you know it, Mommy will be calling, ready for breakfast."

"JJ come in Daddy's bed too?" Lily asked, holding a hand out to her brother. "Monsters not find him here. Us all hide under covers."

Jonas chuckled under his breath and winked at JJ.

JJ scrunched his face. "Uh, yeah. I think I'm gonna pass," he said slowly. "Besides, Jacey is in my room all alone. She's probably scared too. I'll just stay with her. But you'll be just fine now, Lily. So go get under those covers and have sweet dreams."

Jonas put his hand on his son's head and gave it a gentle shake. "Good night, JJ. Sleep well!"

"Kiss for Lily, JJ!" she reminded her brother.

He leaned over and gave his sister a good-night kiss. She in turn gave him a big sloppy one, then giggled.

"Night-night, my JJ. Me love you!"

Mona awoke to whining, then howling. She got out of bed and followed the eerie sounds to the kitchen, where she found poor

Josie under the table, hiding from the storm. Mona glanced at the clock on the stove.

"Oh my, girl. It's three thirty in the morning," she told Josie. "Why did you wander out of the cozy bedroom and come out here?"

She pulled out one of the chairs near the huddled dog, sat down, and stroked Josie's curly fur.

"There now—everything is fine. I know it's a really loud rainstorm. But I bet if I give you a treat, you'll feel much better," she said with a laugh.

Mona got up to search the cupboard for a dog treat. She used it to point toward the bedroom. "Come on, girl. Let's head back to bed."

After one look at the treat, Josie bolted for the bedroom with her mistress close behind. Mona gave Josie her reward, then patted the bed for Josie to jump up. Mona switched off the light, then lay down with Josie nestled into her side. Mona put her hand on the dog's head, falling asleep in exactly that position.

The cavalry of thunder and lightning eventually retreated, and the rain slowly gave up its tempestuous fight. The angry sky gave way to a warm, pleasant breeze that ushered in a lovely Sunday morning.

The first light of dawn produced a golden-orange gleam across the beach, pushing the moon and stars into their daytime hibernation. Ocean waves played havoc with the sand, transporting urchins and other sea life along its constant journey out to sea and back again.

A light and gentle breeze danced along the coastline. A luscious fragrance of honeysuckle permeated the freshness of the early-morning dew. A delicate ballet began with a series of piqué turns and jetés playing in and out of the water.

Then the wind picked up and performed grand jetés around a particular area of beach. Once at her special spot, the lovely breeze whirled in a finale of fouetté turns. The glistening sunrise brought with it new hope of secrets uncovered and the promise of true love's return.

Part Three

Chapter 23

AWAKENINGS

April 22, 2012—Abemly Shores, 8:00 a.m.

CASSIE STIRRED, TURNED, THEN STRETCHED OUT of her fetal sleeping position.

Such a strange dream, she thought as little pieces of memories and images came to her waking mind. But then she bolted upright. *Oh my gosh! That wasn't a dream! Just what the heck happened last night?*

Cassie rushed out of bed, only to trip over a boot that had been left on the floor. *Damn, now I remember . . . Charlie.* She picked up the boot gingerly at first, then she flung it across the room in anger.

"Damn, damn, damn!" she blurted out loud. Instantly, her head started throbbing.

Yawning, Suz dragged herself into Cassie's bedroom and stood in the doorway. "Ah, I see you're awake. But hey—take it easy on the boots. If you don't want them, I know someone who does." With a grin, she picked up the boot and measured it against her foot. "Yep. If I get a few toes shortened, they'll be a perfect fit."

Cassie couldn't help but cackle and shake her head. "You are so funny. Even in the toughest times, you know how to make me laugh! But no, you can't have the boots. I didn't say I was getting rid of them!"

Cassie found the other boot on the floor, sat right down next to it, and held it in her lap.

"Seriously, though, what am I supposed to do now?" she asked. "I feel like my life is on hold in la-la land while I figure out if Charlie really has returned after nine lousy years. Unbelievable! I know I keep saying that, but seriously. I mean, where has he been?"

Suz flopped down on the floor too. She reached out to pat her friend's hand. "Cass," she began, "do you remember what we talked about last night? You decided to talk to him sometime and simply find out what he has to say."

"*Simply?*" Cassie repeated. "Really? There's nothing 'simple' about this situation! It's ridiculous, absurd, preposterous, and all the other ludicrous words I learned in journalism school." She put her hands to her hair, gave it a pull, and let out a little shriek. "I sincerely hope Viv carries wigs, because before this is over, I'm going to pull my hair out!"

Just then, Cassie felt a trickle on her cheek. She wiped at it with her hand, then inspected it. "Blood? Do tell: Why do I have blood on my face?"

"Uh, yeah. About that . . . When you fainted last night, you were holding a bottle of wine and some glasses in your hands. When you went down, you clobbered yourself with the wine bottle, which broke. Hence, the aching head and some bloody cuts to round it out," Suz explained with an apologetic smile.

Cassie went into the bathroom to examine her cuts and bruises in the mirror. "Well, I think I'll live, but I am quite the sight." She walked back into the bedroom and pointed toward the window still covered with cardboard. "Speaking of quite the sight, that must have been some storm last night. I can't believe I slept through it."

"Maybe you couldn't hear the storm outside because there was a bigger storm raging inside," Suz said with a knowing laugh. "I think I cleaned up most of the mess, but you'll need to run a vacuum to catch any more glass I might have missed. And you'll need Jonas to replace that window. And most importantly, you'll need to get Clint reframed!"

Cassie gave Suz a warm smile and hug. "Thank you so much for everything. I'm feeling pretty good now, so I don't think I need a babysitter anymore. I'm sure you have plenty to do at home to get ready for the week."

Suz nodded. "Okay, Cass—as long as you're sure you'll be all right."

"Yes, I'll be fine. Thanks again for being here and helping me through this." Just then, Cassie heard her phone ring. "Oh, there's my phone—I better get it. I'll talk to you later."

As Cassie rushed to answer her phone, Suz gave her a thumbs-up and let herself out.

"Cassie, hi! How are you? It's Savannah," said the familiar voice on the other line. "I just spoke to Jonas. He told me you fainted at the café last night! He said he'd check on you today, but I just had to talk to you myself. Are you feeling better? I don't understand what actually happened."

"Oh my gosh, Savannah—you didn't have to call me while you're on tour! But it's sweet of you to be concerned."

"Of course I'm concerned! You're one of my best friends, and I care about you. So, I heard something about you fainting and falling. What happened?"

"Oh boy. It's a long story. Even I don't fully understand the details at this moment. I promise I'll fill you in once I figure out what's going on. But for now, let's just say something, um, surprised me last night, and down I went. But enough about me," Cassie said, quickly changing the subject. "How are things on the West Coast? Is the tour going well? What's this I hear from Jonas about your music being used for a new movie? How exciting is that!"

Savannah laughed. "Yes, things are good out here. And yes, there is talk about a movie, but it'll be very interesting if that even materializes. For now, I'm just so ready to come home! I miss Jonas and the kids so much—I can't wait to get back to Abemly."

"I can't wait for you to be home too," Cassie agreed. "I'm excited for you to get back so we can talk over coffee at Book Benders. You know, it just isn't the same having coffee there without you. That said, the last time I had coffee, my date, Lily, paid for me." She laughed. "You should have seen her outfit—so adorable. JJ helped her pick it out. You certainly have two wonderful kids!"

Cassie paused as a knock echoed at her door.

"Oh, I hear someone at my door. Sorry, but I should see who it is."

"Sure. No problem! We'll talk later," Savannah said. "Thanks for calling. Bye!"

Cassie quickly hung up, then went to open the door. She found Jonas standing there.

"Jonas! What's up? I actually just got off the phone with Savannah. It was great to talk to her and so nice of her to check in with me."

Jonas smiled, but his face still showed great concern. "First of all, how are you doing? You took a nasty fall last night. We were all really worried about you! I hope Suz took extra good care of you."

"Yes, she did," Cassie assured him. "She had a lot to deal with, though, between me and the storm. As you'll see, we'll need to replace that window! It was a mess—and so was I! Thank goodness for Suz. I sent her home just a bit ago. I figured I'm a big girl and can take care of myself, although I admit she was a great help."

The concern didn't change much on Jonas's face, but now it was mixed with confusion. "Well, I still don't understand what made you faint. But I'm glad you're looking better—except for those cuts, maybe."

Cassie knew she couldn't possibly explain what had happened, so she let his comment slide by. "All that matters is that things are good today. Thanks for caring." Once again, she changed the subject. "Do you need any help downstairs?"

"No, we're fine. Thanks. Oh, but there is someone else concerned about your fall. It's Slim, the singer from last night. I never got to introduce you to him. He's downstairs in the café having breakfast right now, actually. If you feel up to it, come on down."

Cassie had to reach for the doorframe to steady herself.

Jonas eyed her carefully. "Really, you should come downstairs," he gently insisted. "I think you need food. You're starting to look pale and a little faint again. I'll cook up some of your favorite eggs and grits."

Cassie hesitated a few seconds, then cleared her throat. "Ah, I guess food would be good. And I do want to meet Slim. No time like the present," she added for herself more than for Jonas. "I'll be down in a few minutes."

Once Jonas headed back downstairs, Cassie hurried into the bathroom to wash her face and, well, try to look presentable, given her condition. Then she rushed into her bedroom closet. She dug for clothes before she finally stopped in her tracks.

What am I doing? He doesn't give a rip about me—or us, for that matter. So why do I care how I look? She thought for a moment, then lifted her chin smugly. *I know why—because I want him to eat his heart out when he sees me!* But her smugness quickly faded into sadness. *That is, if he even remembers me.*

Cassie finally settled on a pair of jean capris and flip-flops, then she slipped an age-old T-shirt over her head. Glancing at her back in the mirror she saw that the T-shirt read, "Stop 'n' Drop Café—Best Coffee on the Go." She shook her head, wondering why she had kept that old faded yellow shirt anyway. She then grabbed a bandanna off her dresser and tied it around her ponytail as she started cautiously down the stairs. She went in through the kitchen to let Jonas know she was there and to grab a pot of coffee and a cup. She paused to take a deep breath before walking out to the café floor.

Slim was sitting in that corner booth. He was writing something on a napkin.

Cassie tightened her grip on the coffeepot and cup. She took a good, long look at him. The night before, everything had happened so quickly. She really didn't see him clearly before she fainted.

But now she could study him carefully. Cassie walked slowly toward him, contemplating his every movement. His head was bent down, but it still showed waves through his sandy-brown hair, even if it was a bit disheveled. Just then, he gave his head that sexy shake to sweep hair from his eyes . . . those eyes. Cassie gulped as she saw a gleam from those emerald eyes she had gazed into so long ago when she said, "I do." When he raised his head, she needed to steady herself yet again as she caught a glimpse of a telltale bolo around his neck.

She was certain. This wasn't some cowboy who looked and acted like Charlie.

This *was* Charlie.

Chapter 24

INNER AWAKENINGS

April 22, 2012—Abemly Shores, 9:00 a.m.

Perhaps feeling eyes on him, Slim looked up. He grinned.

"Hello, Little Darlin'! Are you gonna share that pot of coffee or drink it all yourself? How are you feeling today? You had a nasty fall last night! When I came over to help, you opened those blue eyes to me for a split second, then passed out again. I hope it wasn't anything I said or did." Displaying that seductive smile, he added, "You're still lookin' a bit pale! You better sit down. I'll pour us a cup of that java."

Slowly and with a deep frown, Cassie headed toward him. As she neared, Slim rose to his feet and presented a bouquet of flowers that had been lying next to him in the booth.

"These are for you. I hope you like yellow."

She looked at the yellow flowers, then down at her very faded yellow T-shirt. She suddenly remembered it had been a gift from Charlie to mark their first date. All these memories were flooding her. But why was Charlie acting as if he didn't remember a thing—including who she was?

Exasperated, Cassie ignored the flowers. She sat down and set the coffeepot between them.

"Are you kidding me? This is ridiculous, Charlie! I know it's you!" she snapped. "But what I don't understand is where you've been for nine years and why you would let me think you were dead. That's just plain cruel! And what about your parents? I mean, what do they think of all this?"

Slim slumped down into the booth as if injured by this unexpected blow. "Hey now—wait just one minute there, Little Darlin'. What's cruel is you comin' over here talkin' about my parents, who are both deceased. What's all this about being dead for nine years? And who, might I ask, is Charlie? I like you fine, but you're throwin' me for a loop, Mizz . . . Mizz . . . I'm sorry. I don't know your name."

Cassie practically lifted herself out of the booth as she slammed her hand on the table. "For your information, the name isn't 'Mizz.' It's actually Cassie. Mrs. Cassie Sands Tanum. I'm your wife—or at least I was until you decided to play dead, Mr. Charles Tanum!"

Tearing up and feeling as if she had a grapefruit stuck in her throat, Cassie tried her best not to cry as she pressed on.

"Why are you doing this to me? You fought so hard for us to be together, but now you won't even acknowledge that you know who I am. This is just absurd! Why are you playing this game with me? Didn't our marriage mean anything to you?"

Slim shook his head, and his eyes grew wider and wider. "Whoa there, Mizz Cassie! You must have me mixed up with someone else! My name is Chuck Houston, and I've never been married."

He closed his eyes now and put his hands to his head, which was beginning to throb a bit. When he opened his eyes again, they pleaded with Cassie.

"Look, I think you're a knockout. I think you have the most amazing big blue eyes I've ever seen. I might be interested in getting to know you better. But I'm still telling you, I've never seen you before last night!" His words were growing louder.

At that moment, Jonas came over with two heaping breakfasts and set them on the table. He was smiling, but it seemed strained.

"Is everything okay over here? Can I get you more coffee or maybe some juice?" He threw a quick glance over his shoulder, then dropped his voice. "Or how about some boxing gloves? It sure sounds like you two strangers have gotten acquainted rather quickly! I'm not sure what's going on here, but seriously—can you keep it a little quieter? Sorry to be the warden, but the other patrons are getting concerned."

Cassie looked around the café. People were indeed eyeing them in confusion.

"I'm so sorry, Jonas," she said. "We promise to eat quietly, and then I'm going to ask 'Slim' here to come upstairs to my apartment."

"Wait just a minute here, ma'am," Slim shot back. "I don't think it's a very good idea for us to be alone in your place just yet."

Cassie let out an angry groan, though as quietly as she could manage. "Do *not* call me 'ma'am'! And believe me, I don't intend on getting cozy with you upstairs! I just have some photos and articles that you have to see."

Jonas hovered at the booth, looking from Cassie to Slim, waiting to see what would happen next.

"Fine," Slim said reluctantly. "We'll eat—quietly—then I'll go upstairs to see whatever you've got that's so important."

Satisfied, Jonas left for the kitchen. The other patrons eventually went back to their breakfasts as the couple in the corner booth ate in silence.

Once finished, Slim followed Cassie to her apartment. When they reached the top of the stairs, Cassie turned to get her key from its hiding place. When she spun back around, Slim was standing even closer to her.

Caught off guard, Cassie found herself staring into those sparkling emerald-green eyes. Her heart definitely skipped a beat. She immediately got woozy and began to sway.

Slim caught her in his arms before she could fall. They held each other for a moment—a very long magical moment before letting go.

"Whoo-wee!" he exclaimed. "What was that? I have to admit, there was a different kind of feeling there." His head throbbed even more now. "Mizz Big Blue Eyes, I think you tripped my trigger. Can I get a glass of water, please? I'm getting one of my headaches, so I need to take my pills."

Cassie ushered him into the apartment. "Have a seat wherever you'd like, Charlie. I'll get you some water."

"I told you, my name's not—" he started, but then he just shrugged as he sat on the couch. "Okay, fine. You want to call me Charlie? Go right ahead. But each time you do, my head hurts worse for some reason!"

Cassie frowned as she went into the kitchen to get some water. "How long have you been having these headaches?" she asked as she handed him the glass.

Slim didn't answer. Instead, he pulled some pills from his pocket and washed them down. Cassie could see the pain on his face.

"So, where are these things you want me to see?" he finally asked, trying to hide his impatience. "Then I'm afraid I have to get going. I'm on a deadline for an article."

Without a word, Cassie retrieved the big album of articles and put it on the coffee table. She just pointed for him to open it.

He flipped through the pages at first. Then he slowed down to trace the name Charlie Tanum with his finger. He did the same with the name Cassie Sands Tanum. After a bit, he began reading the articles and stories.

That was when he broke out in a sweat. It seemed the more he read, the worse his head got. He tried to massage his temples as he turned each page. When he finished, he leaned back on the sofa and closed those tired emerald eyes.

Cassie got up from the couch and disappeared into her bedroom. When she returned, she was wearing the boots he'd bought her so long ago. She hoped to jar his memory. Under her arm, she carried the photo from the nightstand. Taking one look at him sweating and holding his head in agony, she set the photo facedown on the table.

"You don't look so good," she said with worry. "Maybe you should lie down on the floor. I give pretty good back rubs— you probably don't remember. But it may make you feel better."

Slim couldn't explain why, but he proceeded to stretch out on the living room floor, lying on his stomach with his head resting on his crossed arms. For some reason, he was willing to let a complete stranger massage him.

Cassie got down on the floor next to him. She worked on his tense, tight, and very familiar back muscles. She tried to hold back tears welling up in her eyes as she ran her hands over her long-lost husband's neck and shoulders, those wonderful broad shoulders. She used to rest her head on those shoulders to fall asleep.

Charlie, alias Slim, began to relax as she worked. Cassie could feel it in his neck. Oh, how she wanted to lean into him and gently smother him with kisses. She was so close; she could feel the warmth of his body. She wished to hold him even closer, sharing the heat and listening to the familiar beating of his heart.

Why doesn't he know who I am? He must have some sort of total memory loss. I have to find out what happened. Maybe I can jar his memory.

"I have something else for you to see," she said. "It should convince you of who you really are."

She placed the photo next to him. Slim lifted his arms into a push-up position to stare at the picture, then he flipped over on his back and sat up. His eyes were wide as saucers.

"How did you get this picture? Where was it taken? You must have had me superimposed into it or something. But why?" He was frantic now, grabbing the photo off the floor. "Why are you tormenting me with these things? What did I ever do to you?"

He used his palms once again to massage the severe pain in his head. Then he stood up and found his way to the couch, still holding the picture in his hands. As he turned the frame over, he noticed an envelope taped to the back.

He looked at Cassie for approval. When she nodded, he carefully removed and opened it. He slipped a black-and-white image out of the envelope. It was an ultrasound picture. He glanced at it, then at Cassie, whose eyes had become damp and red.

"Is this what I think it is?" he asked, his voice barely a whisper. "But why am I lookin' at it? What's goin' on here?" He shook his head. "I am a freelance writer and part-time singer-songwriter. I have no family and no ties. I'm just a drifter from town to town. I don't mean to be rude, but I just don't understand any of this."

Deep sobs came from Cassie. She got up from the floor and stood near the couch, where Slim sat perplexed.

With her standing there, he got a good look at her boots— then he looked at the photo and did a double take. They were the same boots.

Something happened inside him.

"I don't know why, but something tells me I bought those for you . . ." he said slowly.

"Oh my God, yes! Yes, you did!" Cassie said excitedly. "You told me that if we were going to see your parents in Texas, I had to wear cowboy boots!"

"Texas?" he repeated. It was a question at first. Then he said it again, this time as a statement. "Texas. Yes. I'm from Texas. And there's a ranch with horses . . . horses . . . names like . . . Selly."

Suddenly, Slim grimaced and cradled his head. "Oh man—my head is gonna burst! God, it hurts to say the name. But why?"

Slim could feel something inside him becoming clearer. But the clearer it got, the harder the leprechauns danced in his head. He knew, though, he had to push through.

Still holding the ultrasound picture, he looked into those big blue eyes, now blood red and flooded with tears. He looked at her boots, then back at the picture of a perfectly healthy baby.

"*A girl!*" he shouted. "She . . . she was ours, wasn't she? She was our Little Darlin'."

And then the dam broke.

"Oh my God!" Charlie cried out. "Something happened to her, didn't it? Oh, Cass. And it was my fault—I made you ride! Oh God!"

He scrambled to his feet, nearly knocking over the coffee table. He barely made it to the bathroom in time.

Cassie could only curl up in a ball on the couch, sobbing. She sobbed with devastation for her child, with exhaustion for the fight it took to help Charlie find himself, and with jubilance for finally putting her life back together after nine grueling years.

When Charlie came back into the room, he too had red eyes. He didn't saunter; he walked slowly to the couch. He knelt and embraced his Little Darlin', the love of his life. Finding each other after all this time, the kisses came oh-so sweetly. They rekindled a flame that had prematurely been extinguished so long ago.

He pulled back from the kiss and locked eyes with her. "Cass, you know I would do anything to bring that little girl back, to erase all the bad that has come between us. You believe me, don't you?" he pleaded, tears falling.

Before she could respond, he clamped his eyes shut and continued.

"But I'm sorry—I have to go now. I need time. I'll come back—I promise. I won't be long. I just need . . . time. Please, Little Darlin', try to understand."

He pulled her into a long passionate kiss. And then he was once again gone.

Chapter 25

MIXED-UP MEMORIES

April 22, 2012, 10:30 a.m.—Abemly Shores

CHARLIE RAN DOWN THE STAIRS from the apartment, stopping at the bottom to glance back. He was trying to put in chronological order all the memories that had flooded him in the last thirty minutes. But his head seemed to be in a vice that was tightening by the second! He could also feel a sensation of fluid dripping from his ear. It was making him crazy—and terrified. He'd never felt anything like it before.

Oh, man the pain—the excruciating pain! It just gets worse the more memories I recall. I have to go somewhere so I can think more clearly . . . away from Cassie . . . away from Abemly.

He began running down the boulevard to Gulf's Inn. Then he ran faster when he saw his old rusted green truck. His getaway was in sight! Charlie knew he could think once he was cruisin' on the road out of town.

The ultrasound. Our little girl. Sweat and blood trickled down his clammy neck, though he was oblivious to it. Thoughts began to form in his mind, and they didn't make much sense. *I have to find her for Cassie, for my Little Darlin'. Cassie'll forgive me when I find her! She looks just like her mom, that beautiful blond hair that I fell for on campus.*

Campus? He froze right there on the street as a real memory made its way through the confusing fog. *Where? Which campus? It's snowing. Big white flakes. She's cold, so cold. I have to warm her. Hot drinks, yes. There it is—the Stop 'n' Drop Café! We'll go in. She can be warm!*

Charlie noticed that he was beginning to catch the attention of onlookers. He decided to just nod politely and reach up to tip his hat—which wasn't there.

Where in the hell is my Stetson? He glanced back at the café up the street. *Damn. I left it on the table. But I can't go back till I find our little girl.*

He finally reached his oasis—the old green truck had never looked so good. Jumping in, he subconsciously tapped the bolo hanging on the rearview mirror. Taking a deep, cleansing breath, he started down Main Street, passing Book Benders.

Suddenly, he spotted a little blond-haired girl sitting on a bench, hugging and kissing a dog.

Oh golly. Why is she alone? Where is Cassie?

Turning the truck around at the first corner, he lost sight of the child. He pulled over and parked on the side of the boulevard. He wiped his face with his shirt, then pulled back out and kept driving.

Chapter 26

DO DREAMS COME TRUE?

April 22, 2012, 10:45 a.m.—Abemly Shores

CASSIE SAT CLUTCHING THE FRAMED PHOTO in disbelief. She gently picked up the ultrasound image and carefully slipped it back into its envelope, attaching it to the back of the frame. Staring at the photo, she didn't know what to think or do.

Oh my God, she thought. *What just happened? My Charlie, my husband, the love of my life, has miraculously reappeared after nine years—but now he's vanished again? No way! He can't just walk back into my life for a few hours and then disappear again!*

It all left her with a mix of emotions that made her want to scream. She was ecstatic to see Charlie alive, yet at the same time, she was so angry she wanted to kill him. And she was still left wondering what he'd been doing all these years.

On top of it, now she was worrying about his debilitating headaches. What could be causing them? Did they have anything to do with his amnesia? Did something cause him to lose his memory shortly after he had left Cassie in Philly? She knew he had been on a secret assignment. Had he gotten hurt somehow?

Wiping the dampness from her eyes, she jumped up to splash water on her face. "That's it," she said out loud, looking in the bathroom mirror. "He's not getting away this time!"

She went out to grab her keys. This time, she would make sure she was there to help Charlie through his pain. She'd be there to catch him when he fell.

We've been through too much to not fight to be together.

She got in her car and began driving up and down the streets, trying to spot Charlie. Where would he go to get peace and quiet? Maybe near Abemly Sound or possibly the beach—those were calming places.

Cassie decided to go to the beach first. Getting out of her car, she headed toward the ocean, stopping to slip off her shoes so she could walk more easily in the sand. But seeing mainly families having picnics, and not recognizing anyone who resembled her husband, she turned back and went to the car.

Her next stop was Abemly Sound. Cassie pulled the car up near Waterfront Park and proceeded to walk to the path near the water's edge. She walked on for a bit, then decided to check the marina. No luck. Charlie wasn't anywhere to be found.

Cassie got back in her car and continued searching, stopping everywhere and anywhere she could think of. Then she made another loop, stopping again at each place.

When she returned to the park, Cassie smiled when she noticed JJ and Lily with Jacey. They were playing hide-and-seek.

Lily was "hiding" in nearly plain sight behind a bench. But being the good big brother that he was, JJ made it seem that he couldn't find her.

Then Cassie noticed a woman sitting at another bench. She had a book in her hands, though she wasn't reading. She was watching the kids. Intently. Something about it made Cassie's smile turn into a tight line.

Perhaps the woman sensed someone watching her in turn, so she gave a sideways glance in Cassie's direction. When they made eye contact, the woman quickly opened her book and pretended to be reading.

That's odd, Cassie thought.

Part of her wanted to go say hi to the kids, but there wasn't time for that now. She had to keep looking for Charlie.

Hours passed, and evening arrived. Cassie thought—or at least hoped—maybe Charlie had gotten tired and gone back to her apartment. She hurried home, anticipating him waiting at the top of the stairs for her.

She had nothing but disappointment.

She unlocked the door, went inside, sat down, took off her boots, and picked up the album he'd left on the table.

Chapter 27

HAUNTING MELODY

April 22, 2012, 7:00 a.m. PT—Los Angeles

JUST TWO MORE CITIES AND FOUR MORE PERFORMANCES—then Savannah would be heading home to her family. She couldn't wait to sit on her porch, take in the scent of the ocean, and feel the evening breeze dance through her hair.

After calling Cassie, Savannah took her morning run along the river near her hotel. She delighted in imagining the homecoming scene with her loving family and close friends in Abemly Shores.

She thought of one friend in particular, Mona. She was such a history buff. Throughout the tour, Savannah had compiled pictures and information about the historic theaters she'd performed in. She was eager to share it all with her good friend.

When she reached the halfway point of her run, she stopped long enough to stretch her arms above her head, then reach down to her toes. It was almost time to befriend yet another piano for yet another rehearsal at yet another theater. She turned to head back to the hotel, pushing herself at a faster pace.

Savannah helped herself to a complimentary apple and cup of coffee in the lobby before heading to her room. She had skipped breakfast before her run, something she usually tried to avoid.

Savannah enjoyed a quick shower, but then something odd happened. When she grabbed for a towel, it slipped through her hand. Simultaneously, she herself slipped on the wet tile. She nearly hit the floor.

At that second, a horrible sinking feeling came over her. Something was wrong. Maybe at home.

Very slowly, she picked up the towel with tingling, trembling hands. She wrapped it around her, then went to sit down on the vanity bench near the sink.

No, I can't think like that. Nothing is wrong. For Pete's sake, I just spoke to Jonas and the kids this morning. Everything was fine.

She took a deep breath. There had to be a rational explanation for this strange feeling that had overcome her.

Maybe I overdid it this morning. I know better than to run on an empty stomach. I'm probably just dehydrated.

Somewhat convinced, she got dressed, finished her apple, downed a bottle of water, grabbed one for the road, then went off to rehearse.

Walking into a silent auditorium was always a near-religious experience for Savannah. She was awestruck as the thick majestic doors closed solidly behind her. She stopped immediately, closed her eyes, and took a deep breath. She drew in the familiar aroma of the theater—the scent of age-old polished wood floors. She then opened her eyes to admire the regal carvings covering both the walls and ceiling of the old theater. Finally, she gazed at the worn leather seats, subtle and cracked like priceless mosaics.

The warm, welcoming smell and glow of the stage lights sent shards of electricity through her back, over her shoulders, then down to her hands. The excitement and profound emotion of standing alone in the great theater was overwhelming. Tears of joy and gratitude slid down her cheek. Each tear was like dew clinging to a blade of grass on an early-spring morn.

As a bride walking to her groom, Savannah glided down the aisle to the magnificent grand piano perched on the stage. She couldn't wait to feel the ivory keys mold to her touch. Stopping the moment she reached the stage, she closed her eyes once again and took in the silent greatness of the moment.

From out of nowhere, she heard a beautiful but haunting melody. She blinked open her eyes, expecting to see someone playing the piano. But there was no one. The piano stood at attention, waiting only for her hands to caress it. She could no longer hear the melody, though it was still fresh in her mind.

Shaking off the chill that ran up her spine, she sat at the piano and set up her music. She began by running scales to warm up her fingers and become acquainted with the instrument. As she played, she tried not to think about the melody that had floated through the air and into her head.

When she was ready to start practicing in earnest, Savannah decided to grab her water bottle before settling down for what would likely be hours. With a smile, Savannah gifted her new cohort with a beautiful glissando.

"I'll be right back," she said aloud.

Savannah pushed the bench back and stood to leave. But as soon as she turned her back to the piano, she swore she heard trills! However faintly, she heard music—the same haunting melody from before.

She whipped her head around to stare at the piano. It sat at attention, its keys at rest.

Before she could even catch her breath, another sound made her swing her head around. This time, it was toward those magnificent ornate doors. A phenomenal gust of wind forced them open.

For a second, there was silence. But then the floorboards started creaking, groaning. There was a scurry of something, perhaps in the balcony. That haunting melody grew stronger and stronger.

Savannah whirled around once again to the piano, expecting to see someone making the black and whites march and dance. There was nothing, no one. Yet the music continued to wind and glide through the theater, entertaining those empty time-worn seats.

Heart pounding, Savannah ran down into the aisles, where the ghostly audience remained silently focused on the performance floating about. The lights flickered, then went dark. Engulfed in the blackness of the theater, Savannah could hear leather cracking on the seats around her.

Suddenly, all the lights came on. The seat cushions banged up and down. The melody became more intense. Something raced and leaped in the aisles. A gust of wind painfully sobbed as it swirled around Savannah and spun her toward the stage.

Paralyzed, Savannah watched as every spotlight swept back and forth, forming what appeared as a message on the massive curtain framing the piano.

HOME.

NOW.

HELP!

Chapter 28

TAXI, ANYONE?

April 22, 2012, 9:15 a.m. PT—Los Angeles

IN A STATE OF DISBELIEF, Savannah flew out of the haunted theater. Not wanting to even glance back, she hailed a cab. Almost instantly, one appeared at the curb before her.

"Please—you have to get me to the Grand Hyatt as fast as you can!" she told the driver through her hysterics.

The driver was an older gentleman. His kindly face filled with concern. "Yes, ma'am. I understand." With determination and skill, he began maneuvering through traffic.

Trembling uncontrollably, Savannah punched every number on her cell phone that she could think of. Home, the café, Mona, Cassie, the Sillses. Each went straight to voice mail.

"Oh my God—why won't anybody answer?" she cried aloud.

Savannah closed her eyes and tried to catch her breath. The whole episode at the theater, even the strange feeling this morning in the shower—she now understood it was all a sign.

"Charlotte . . ." she whispered, her eyes still closed.

As unbelievable as it seemed, she knew it was a sign from Charlotte. In some way, Charlotte was telling her something horrible had happened at home.

Gripped with fear and dread, Savannah fell into a trance. Next thing she knew, the driver was addressing her.

"Ma'am?" he said, finally getting her attention. "We're here." His eyes were still full of fatherly concern. "Is there anything else I can do? Do you perhaps need a ride somewhere else?"

"Yes!" Savannah almost shouted. "I—I—I need to get to the airport. It'll take just a second to get my suitcase. Could you wait for me?"

"Absolutely," he answered without hesitation. He was calm, yet his worry still showed in his wrinkled face. Something about him allowed Savannah to steady her breath and nerves.

With resolve, she nodded to him, then raced inside the hotel. Inside her room, it took only a few moments to gather the few stray belongings into her suitcase. She typically never unpacked while on tour, seeing as she hopped from hotel to hotel nearly every other day.

With one hand, she packed. With the other, she tried calling anyone back in Abemly. Still, no one answered. It was so strange that she couldn't get through to anyone. She thought about texting, but there was no time.

I have to keep my wits about me. All I can do is get to the airport ASAP and just hope that everyone is safe and sound.

Suitcase in tow, she ran back to the waiting cab. Without a word, the driver headed for the airport, expertly slicing his way through traffic once again.

Savannah left a checkout call with the hotel, then called the airline.

"I need to be on the first flight that will get me as close to Abemly Shores, South Carolina, as possible," she told the ticket agent, her voice wavering. "It's an emergency!"

Miraculously, there was one seat left on a flight to Charleston that was due for takeoff soon. There were only minutes to spare, so the agent promised they'd hold the flight for her.

By the time Savannah had finished booking her ticket, the driver was pulling into the curbside drop-off area at the airport. He hurried out to get her door and help her with her suitcase.

"Wait—I need to pay," she said, digging into her purse for her wallet.

"No," the driver said firmly, shaking his head. "I'm just glad I could help."

For a moment, Savannah just stared at the driver with tears in her eyes. At perhaps the worst moment in her life, here was this helpful, caring man.

He smiled reassuringly at her. "It'll be all right," he said with utmost sincerity. "Everything will be all right."

Savannah managed a small smile back, then rushed into the airport.

Chapter 29

ANGEL IN THE AIR

April 22, 2012, 10:00 a.m. PT—Los Angeles

ONLY MINUTES BEFORE TAKEOFF, Savannah finally made it to her seat on the plane heading to Charleston. Out of breath, she pushed her carry-on bag under the seat in front of her, then pulled out her cell phone to try calling home again.

This time, she saw that a text had come through from Cecilia. All it said was, "Please, Savannah—come home ASAP. You need to be here!"

Savannah gasped. It was true, then. Something horrible *had* happened. But what? She dialed Cecilia's number, eager yet terrified to finally get some answers.

In the next seat, a grandmotherly woman eyed Savannah with concern. For a second, she turned to Savannah, as if to say something.

Just then, a flight attendant came by. "I'm sorry, ma'am," she said to Savannah in a polite voice, "but cell phones must be off and stowed for takeoff."

Savannah's eyes filled with panic, and she shook her head. "Oh, please—can I use it for just one second?" she pleaded, trying to keep her composure. "There's a family emergency!"

The flight attendant placed a kind hand on Savannah's shoulder. "I'm so sorry. I truly am. But we can't have cell phone interference when we're in the air. But don't worry—we'll be landing in six short hours."

On the outside, Savannah nodded. On the inside, she let out a silent scream. Her head was pounding so hard she thought the older woman in the next seat might hear it.

Oh my God—six "short" hours? How will I ever get through this flight without losing my mind? I'll go crazy! Something has happened at home, and I can't even call or text to find out what!

It was just too much to take. Savannah tried to catch her breath, but she couldn't. She started hyperventilating. The flight attendant had started to walk away, but she quickly stopped and returned to Savannah's side.

"Ma'am, I'm going to get you a cold washcloth and some water. In the meantime, please take slow, deep breaths."

As the flight attendant hurried away, the woman sitting next to Savannah reached over. She patted Savannah's hand.

"Is there something I can do to help, dear? You're as white as a ghost."

Savannah turned to the woman and shook her head. Just looking at her kind face seemed to have a calming effect. The woman's calm, supportive presence almost reminded Savannah of the cab driver's.

Before she knew it, Savannah's breaths were slowing down. By the time the flight attendant returned, Savannah was breathing normally again.

"Thank you," she said to the flight attendant as she took the water and placed the washcloth against her forehead. "And thank *you*," she said to the woman next to her.

Savannah took several deep breaths, then drank some water. She leaned back in her seat and closed her eyes. She had to calm herself down. Even if she could call someone right now, she'd be no help to anyone in her present state of mind.

The cool washcloth definitely helped clear her head. *Whatever has happened at home has happened*, she told herself matter-of-factly. *There's nothing I can do about it now. I can do nothing but get home as soon as possible.*

She took another long drink from her water, then settled back again with her eyes closed. She hoped she would relax if she relived all the wonderful things that had happened in her life during the past six years.

Savannah stirred at the sound of a voice.

"Good evening, everyone. This is Captain Evans, your pilot. I hope you're having an enjoyable flight as we continue on to Charleston. We're a little over an hour from landing. If there's anything we can do to make you more comfortable, please let us know. We will be experiencing some turbulence for the next twenty to thirty minutes. So, for now, buckle up, sit back, and relax."

Savannah opened her eyes, not even realizing she had dozed off. Actually, she had dozed off for quite some time! She could hardly believe they'd be landing in about an hour.

As she stretched, she felt someone lightly touch her arm. She turned to see the woman in the next seat smiling ever-so politely.

"Hello, dear. I hope you're feeling better."

"Yes, a little better. Thank you," Savannah replied.

She sipped on her water while staring out the window at the cloud cover. She wondered once again what was going on in her peaceful little town of Abemly Shores. But this time, she accepted that she had to wait until they landed to learn more.

With only an hour left to go now, she decided to pass the time with some conversation. "Are you on your way home?" she asked the woman next to her. "Or are you going on vacation somewhere?"

"I'm going to visit my son and daughter-in-law and their three children," the woman replied happily. "I'm so looking forward to seeing them. My new granddaughter was born two weeks ago."

With shaky hands, she reached into her purse and took out a small photo book to share with Savannah.

"I wanted to see her sooner. Normally, my husband and I would have driven out. We don't like flying. But my husband has been ill lately, so he finally decided to put me on a plane myself. Here I am, flying—whether I like it or not!" She smiled and chuckled nervously.

As if on cue, the plane jostled with turbulence. The woman shuddered. Savannah was the one this time to reach out with a gentle hand to her shoulder.

"Thank you!" the woman said with a sigh. "Just talking to you makes me feel less nervous! But enough about me. I see you're wearing a wedding band, so I assume you're married. Do you have any children?"

Savannah could tell the woman was respectfully not asking about the family emergency outright. She obviously didn't want to pry, but her warm smile encouraged Savannah to speak freely.

"As a matter of fact, yes," Savannah said after collecting herself for a second. "I'm married to the man of my dreams, and we have two wonderful children. JJ is fourteen and looks just like his dad. He's the best son I could have ever wished for. And then our curly blond little Lily will be three this July. She was a spectacular surprise. She's the light of all our lives! She thinks her big brother is her hero, and he thinks his little sister is his very own fairy princess. Me, I'm a jazz pianist. I've been on tour for a few weeks now. I miss them so much. I just can't wait to get home to our little cottage in Abemly Shores."

Savannah wiped a tear from her eye and shivered. "*Brr!* I just got a chill right down to my toes. It's so cold all of a sudden, don't you think?"

"That's odd—I'm feeling a bit warm and stuffy myself. Though that's probably because of my hot flashes!" the woman said, giggling. "But if you're cold, you best warm yourself up. Should we ask for a blanket?"

"Actually," Savannah said, "I think I have a sweatshirt."

She dug under the seat for her carry-on. As she lifted a sweatshirt out of the bag, something fell out of the pocket.

"Oh," the woman exclaimed. "Something fell. It's there under your foot."

Savannah was surprised to feel warmth resonating next to her foot. *What in the world?* she wondered as she reached down.

The minute her hand touched the object, she knew! She felt the comforting warmth in her fingers as she picked it up. Immediately, she stroked the telltale jagged crack in the center. It was the white stone. The stone Jacey had found on the beach days before Savannah left on her tour.

I had it with me all this time and didn't know? But what is it trying to tell me? Why is it so warm?

Suddenly, Savannah couldn't hold it back any longer. The feeling of panic and dread overtook her once again.

"Please help me!" she beseeched the woman. Her words spilled as fast as her tears. "Something is very wrong at home, but I don't know what! I can't get ahold of anyone!"

The woman took Savannah's hand in hers. "Oh, I'm so sorry, dear. What can I do to help? Perhaps I can stay with you until your family comes to pick you up at the airport?"

Savannah shook her head wildly. "No one will be there—they don't know I'm on this flight! I don't even know how I'll get home to Abemly Shores!"

Savannah felt her breaths speed up. She couldn't control them.

The woman squeezed Savannah's hand, getting her attention. "I have an idea, dear. My son is picking me up at the airport. I think Abemly Shores is on our way to his home. I'm sure he'd be more than happy to give you a ride."

Gulping for air, Savannah nodded and tried to pull herself together. With one hand, Savannah clung to this kind woman. With her other hand, she still clenched the white stone. Her breaths slowed.

"Really?" Savannah finally managed to say. "That would be so kind of you and your son. I just can't thank you enough!"

"Ladies and gentlemen," a voice broke in, "this is Captain Evans, hoping you've had a pleasant flight. We should have you on the ground in Charleston in about twenty minutes, which will be an on-time arrival. Have a good evening, and thank you for flying with us."

The women looked at each other and smiled, both relieved to finally be at their destination.

"I never introduced myself," the woman said. "My name is Marge."

"I'm Savannah. And I'm very fortunate to have sat next to you today."

"Well, I'm also fortunate. I honestly don't know how I would have gotten through that turbulence on my own! I guess you could say we're quite the pair in the air!"

Marge let out a much more relaxed laugh and patted Savannah's hand again.

Chapter 30

LILY!

April 22, 2012, 7:00 p.m.—Charleston, South Carolina

AS THE PLANE CAME TO A STOP AT THE GATE, Savannah attempted to pull herself together. She zipped up her sweatshirt and tapped on the stone before depositing it back in her pocket. Then she and her new friend, Marge, walked off the plane together.

"Honestly, I don't want to trouble you and your son," Savannah said with a nervous smile. "I'm sure you want to get to those beautiful grandchildren as soon as possible. Why don't I just try calling Jonas again to see if he can pick me up?"

"Honestly," Marge echoed as she touched Savannah's hand, "I'm sure it'll be no problem to give you a ride. Besides, you'll get there much more quickly this way. So, it's settled! Now let's gather our luggage and find my son."

"Thank you so much," Savannah said, giving Marge's hand a squeeze.

The women walked through the terminal, with Savannah busy on her phone, trying to reach someone, anyone. Once again, all the lines went to voice mail. She sighed and tried to stay calm.

When they met up with Marge's son, he was more than happy to help Savannah get home to Abemly Shores. He put their luggage in the car, and they drove out of the airport parking ramp.

As they merged onto the highway, Savannah suddenly felt a sharp pain in her chest—as if being pierced by an arrow! She fell back on the seat just as they passed underneath an information sign over the highway. It appeared to be blinking directly at her.

AMBER ALERT
2-YEAR-OLD FEMALE

Thoughts rushed at Savannah at once. *The sign at the theater. Home. Now. Help! The wind. The breeze. Charlotte. She's always near. Watching over us. Home. Now. Help!*

"Oh my God!" she shrieked. "Lily! My baby! Someone has her! *No!* Please don't hurt her! Oh God, please help my little girl!"

Startled by the screams, Marge turned to the back seat.

"Savannah—what is it? What's wrong?"

But now Savannah sat in a semiconscious state, staring at the white stone she kneaded between her fingers. Tears flowed from her eyes, draining down to her sweatshirt and turning it a putrid shade of green.

"Charlotte," Savannah mumbled to herself and the stone. "The wind. The breeze. The message in the theater."

Marge gave her son a pleading look. "She needs help!" she whispered. "Something is happening with her family. Maybe it has something to do with that Amber Alert. There, up ahead—I see a police station. We have to pull over now! They'll know what to do."

Within moments, they were helping Savannah out of the car and into the station. They were ushered in to see an officer immediately. Savannah could barely form words, so Marge spoke on her behalf.

"She was in LA but suddenly had to rush home," Marge explained as best she could. "She said she somehow knew there was a family emergency. Someone named Charlotte messaged her about it or something. I don't really understand," Marge admitted, shaking her head. "Anyway, then she became distraught when she saw the Amber Alert sign out on the highway just now. I'm concerned the abducted child is her daughter, Lily."

The officer tried to conceal his reaction, but his eyes widened. "What's your daughter's full name?" he asked Savannah directly.

"Lily . . . Marie . . . Beckman," she managed to say very slowly.

The officer frowned. "I'm sorry, ma'am, but yes—I can confirm that is the identity of the missing child."

Everyone braced for Savannah's reaction, but there was none. She was frozen, other than her fingers running over the stone. It was almost as if she hadn't heard—or couldn't comprehend—the news.

"Who is this Charlotte?" the officer asked, looking from Savannah to Marge. "How did she know the child was in danger? The Amber Alert was only recently posted. How did Charlotte know this information ahead of time? How can we get hold of her? She may have pertinent information. We definitely need to speak with her about Lily."

Suddenly, Savannah came out of her semitrance, trembling and crying out loud. "My baby—my *Lily*!" She jumped out of her chair and grabbed the officer's sleeve. "You have to help me find my sweet little girl! God, she must be so afraid! She doesn't even have her big brother to help her. He loves her so much—this must be killing him! And Jonas!" She was now screaming. "Where is Jonas? I need to talk to my husband!"

Savannah's knees buckled underneath her. Just before she collapsed out of consciousness, she slipped into the arms of a tall, slim man with black hair and desperately sad dark eyes.

Chapter 31
CHARLOTTE?

April 22, 2012, 8:00 p.m.—Outside Charleston

WITH THE OFFICER'S GUIDANCE, Jonas carried Savannah to a room in the back of the police station. He laid her gently on the cot reserved for officers working overnight shifts. She was shivering and delirious when he covered her with a thin blanket.

"Lily. My little Lily," she repeated over and over in a drowning voice.

He pulled up a chair to sit next to her, then he leaned in to kiss her cheek. His tears mingled with hers. Jonas sat for a moment, watching the pain emanating from every pore of his wife's being. This woman—the mother of his beautiful, tiny, missing daughter—was paralyzed by the shock that something so horrible was happening to them.

Touching her clammy hand, he whispered, "We will find her—we will bring our Lily home. Our family will be complete again."

Tears flowed like a waterfall over his cheekbones, then dripped from his strong, square chin onto that thin blanket covering his ghostly pale soul mate.

He felt a gentle hand on his shoulder and turned to see Marge looking at him with deep compassion through her damp eyes. He put his finger to his lips and then nodded toward Savannah. Marge nodded back, understanding.

Jonas adjusted the blanket before he stood to follow Marge into the other room. He left the door ajar in case Savannah woke.

"You must be Jonas," Marge said softly. "I'm Marge. I met Savannah on the plane, and my son and I were bringing her home when she saw the Amber Alert sign . . ." Her words trailed off.

"Marge, I am so indebted to you for everything you have done to help my wife. Oh, and many thanks to your son as well for getting her here safely."

"But how did you know where to find us—at this station, I mean?" Marge asked, looking very perplexed. "I thought Savannah said she hadn't been able to get in touch with anyone. So it's a miracle that you found us, let alone were right there to catch her when she fainted!"

"Actually, I just somehow knew to call the airlines and inquire about the LA flight coming in tonight. I'm not sure how I picked that one. I just had a feeling about it. And then when I was driving to the airport, I knew the plane had landed and that I missed her. But for some unknown reason, I was drawn to this station. I thought maybe I'd ask if they had any information about my little girl." Jonas paused to marvel at it all. "Maybe it is a miracle."

"Did that woman, Charlotte, have anything to do with you getting here? I don't quite understand all the details, but apparently she was able to reach Savannah in LA to tell her something was wrong at home."

Jonas stared in shock. He had no idea how this helpful stranger knew about Charlotte—or how Charlotte had "reached" Savannah. But he trusted it wasn't a coincidence. His dear Charlotte was most definitely at work here. It actually made him smile.

"Maybe—maybe Charlotte did direct me to find Savannah, somehow. Now, if she could only help us find Lily." His smile faded. He sighed. "Again, thank you for everything. But please—you don't need to stay any longer. Besides, I can tell you came to visit your family. You really should go."

Marge hugged Jonas. "I wish you all the best." She reached into her purse and pulled out a card. "Here's my phone number. Please let me know if I can be of help, and please keep me posted about your progress with the search." She gave him the card, then took his free hand in hers tightly. "Jonas, I will be holding your family in my thoughts. Only good things will come to you and your family. I *know* it."

Just then, Marge's son appeared with Savannah's luggage. He too wished Jonas well and shook hands. Jonas walked with them to the door, then waved as they exited to the parking lot.

Jonas turned next to the officer at the front desk. "While I have a chance to ask, do you happen to have any more information about our daughter?"

"I'm sorry, Mr. Beckman," the officer said, his eyes sympathetic but determined. "There's been no word yet. We're still not sure what happened—she may have wandered off or she may have been abducted. But I can guarantee we will not stop until we find her. We have patrols out within a twenty-five-mile radius of Abemly Shores searching for her."

Jonas walked back to Savannah. As he neared the door, he could hear her stirring. She was sitting up, shaking, and staring into space as he knelt down next to her. She reached her arms around him, hugging him tightly.

"Savannah, we'll find her. I promise we will find our little Lily. She'll be just fine."

She has *to be*, he added to himself.

"Are you steady enough for us to drive back to Abemly?" he asked.

Instantly, Savannah's fog seemed to clear. "Yes," she said decidedly. "We must go home now. Tell me everything—what happened? Where was she? Why wasn't anyone with her? Where is JJ? Is he okay? Maybe she's with him?"

"JJ is at home with John and Cecilia. Your folks had just gotten to the house when I left for the airport." He took Savannah's hands and lifted her up from the cot. "Let's get going, though. I'll fill you in on what I know in the car."

Once in the car and on their way back home, Jonas took a deep breath. "Lily kept asking to go to the park, but I was busy with the café. I suggested she and JJ take Jacey down to Waterfront Park for a bit. I even told her to ask JJ to play hide-and-seek. You know how she loves to hide and then how she giggles that wonderful giggle of hers when he . . . when he . . ." Choking up, Jonas wiped at his eyes before he could finish. "When he finds her."

Jonas suddenly gripped the steering wheel in anger.

"Oh, it's all my fault, Savannah! I'm so sorry! I never should have let her go!"

"No, Jonas—it's not your fault! I should be home with our children instead of traveling all over the country!"

Savannah was red faced with tears pouring down her cheeks. She reached over to seize one of Jonas's hands, squeezing it tightly. Together, they cried for their little girl.

After a few moments, Savannah let out a sigh, trying to compose herself. "I just knew something was wrong," she said quietly. "The strangest thing was that this morning, something happened while I was rehearsing alone at the theater. It was eerie—as if the theater had come alive. There was a force or presence that actually warned me and told me to go home." She paused. "I think it was Charlotte."

Jonas nodded. "You know, ever since JJ was a little boy, he's always said his mom has been looking out for us. Well, this is one time I sure as hell hope she is!"

Savannah tried to smile. "I'm hopeful too. There have been a lot of odd coincidences lately that make me think she's around, helping us."

With that, she took the stone out of her pocket and rubbed it.

Jonas glanced at the stone from the corner of his eye. "What the—?" he immediately said. "Let me see that."

Taking the stone, he examined it as best he could while driving. He felt its warmth and recognized the jagged line through its center.

"I can't believe it. I don't know if you even realized it at the time, but we tossed a stone into Abemly Sound on our wedding day. This is the same exact stone—I know it. I didn't show you the stone that day because I didn't know how to explain that it's also the same exact stone I found on the beach the day Charlotte died. That day too, I threw it in the ocean, gifting it to her. And now *you* found it? Where? How?"

Jonas handed back the stone. Savannah sat in silence for a moment as a chill ran down her spine. Finally, she could speak.

"Actually, Jacey found it during a run on the beach before I left for the tour. I didn't think much of it at first, but there was something about the jagged pink crack down the center and the perfect round shape that made me want to keep it. So I put it in my sweatshirt pocket and forgot about it—until it fell out on the plane today. When I picked it up, it was warm, almost hot to the touch. It made me feel like there was something very wrong at home. Between that and the presence at the theater, I just knew something had happened."

Savannah's eyes filled with fear as thoughts of their little Lily flooded her mind.

"It was a sign, a message. All of it was. It proves that Charlotte can help us—she can guide us to get Lily back."

He squeezed her hand, which still held the stone.

Chapter 32

DREAMS OR NIGHTMARES?

April 22, 2012, 9:15 p.m.—Lauderville, South Carolina

CHARLIE WAS SPRAWLED ACROSS A BED in a dumpy motel about twenty minutes outside of Abemly Shores. He'd been there for hours. When he'd first arrived at the motel, blood occasionally dripped from his ear, and the ringing in his head was intolerable. He downed pills till the pain in his head went numb, then he passed out on the bed.

As the hours passed, dreams kept going through his head about horses and a little girl wearing very large cowboy boots. The boots were almost to her hips and heavy. She was trying to run, but she kept falling because the boots were holding her back. Then she stepped in a type of mud—quicksand! He tried to reach out to help her. She kept sinking, but he wouldn't let go.

"No . . ." he said in his sleep.

Suddenly, he woke with a start, dripping wet from sweat.

Oh man, he thought. *What a horrible dream.*

The small window over his bed rattled, then blew open, inviting in a passel of leaves. They drifted and fell upon the small desk.

Charlie rose to his feet and stumbled to the desk. Everything on the desk was covered in leaves except an advertisement for a Waffle House restaurant a few miles away. He squinted to take a better look at the ad. It said the restaurant was open all night.

Waffle House sounds good. I haven't had much to eat today. I suppose I should get some food. And maybe a cup of java, he added after throwing a wary glance at the one-cup coffee maker on the desk. *I don't have the foggiest clue how that thing works!*

Chapter 33
ADOPTION

April 22, 2012, 9:15 p.m.—Lauderville

Jack returned from the store with a car seat, just as Chey had asked. When he walked into the small two-bedroom bungalow, she was humming a soft song to a child whimpering and struggling in her arms.

She patted the child's hand. "*Sh*, now. It'll be all right."

Jack still couldn't believe it. When he had returned home from one of his shifts, Chey had an amazing surprise for him: she said the adoption agency had stopped by during the day to bring them a child. Her name was Eden.

It almost sounded too good to be true. In an instant, they were parents! But Jack didn't know much about how the adoption process worked. All he knew was that Chey had waited for so long to finally fulfill her dream of being a mother. She looked so overjoyed. He didn't care about how it happened.

"How's the little one doin'?" Jack asked.

With shining eyes, Chey looked up at her husband and then back to the little blond girl, who seemed so scared. "She'll be just fine once she knows how much we love her. Don't ya think, Jack? She'll grow to love us too, right?"

Jack walked over and took his wife's hand. "Yes, our pretty little Eden will learn to love us as much as we love her. It sure was a nice surprise that the adoption agency came through like this. I guess I didn't expect it would all happen so quick. I mean, they didn't even tell us they were coming."

Chey nodded quickly. "Yes, yes. It was all very quick. But they said it was urgent she find a home. You know"—she dropped her voice—"because of the accident."

Jack nodded knowingly. The adoption agency had told Chey that Eden's parents had recently died in a horrible accident. While that was incredibly sad, Jack couldn't help but feel incredibly happy to provide this little girl with a new home. He leaned over to give Chey a peck on the cheek.

"Hey, Jack—or should I say, Daddy?" she added with a grin. "I like calling you that, now that you are one! So, Daddy, I think Eden is hungry. But we don't have much food in the house right now. How about you splurge and take your new family out for a late supper? Kind of a 'welcome home' celebration for Eden."

"I would be obliged to take my beautiful wife and new daughter out for a celebration. I got a little overtime pay from Jonas—"

"Daddy!" the child suddenly cried out.

"Ha! Look at that," Jack said with a huge smile. "She's already calling me Daddy!"

"No!" the girl screamed. "*Jonas* my daddy! I want my daddy!" She hit her hands on the bed and kept shouting, "I want my daddy!"

Jack frowned. "Poor child doesn't seem to understand what happened to her parents."

Chey gave him a sweet smile, but then put a finger to her lips. "No need to discuss her poor dead parents," she whispered. "Let's just get on with the celebration!"

She stood up, bringing the now-crying child to her feet. Chey hugged her husband, then gave him a rather generous kiss on the mouth before they led Eden out to the car.

"Thank you for picking up a car seat for her. Safety is so important. And we only want the best for our little girl. Isn't that right, Jack?"

"Mm hm," he grunted as he set up the car seat.

Chey tucked a blond curl behind the child's ear and wiped away a tear. The child tried to squirm away from her. When Chey kissed her cheek, the girl slapped at her own face, where she had been kissed.

"No, no, no! I want *my* mommy!"

"Sweetie, I am your mommy now. I love you so much," she said patiently, smiling at the small angry child.

They drove to the nearest restaurant, which happened to be Waffle House. Jack parked the car and helped take Eden out of her seat. The girl fought, kicking and batting at him. Jack just tried to stay calm. He could only imagine how difficult it had to be for this little child to start a new life after losing her parents. It would take some time, but she would come to love them, just as Chey said.

So Jack put on a happy face as he and Chey each took one of the girl's hands. She continued to fight against them, but they managed to walk into the restaurant looking like the proud parents they were. They chose a booth near the window so the child could watch the cars going by.

"Sweetheart, would you like pancakes or waffles?" Chey asked the girl. "You must like bacon. Everyone likes bacon. We'll even get you an extra order. How will that be?" She gave her new daughter's cheek a little pinch.

The child slapped at Chey's hand. "No pinch! No touch!" she shouted. "You not my mommy! I want *my* mommy! *Now!*"

There weren't many people in the restaurant at that hour, but the few who were there were staring at them. They had puzzled but concerned expressions, as if trying to make sense of the situation. In particular, the man sitting at the counter behind them kept turning his head.

"Everyone is watching us. Can't you quiet her down?" Jack asked under his breath. He nervously rose to his feet. "I'm going to the john. Maybe you can calm her down by the time I get back!"

Chapter 34
WAFFLE HOUSE EXCITEMENT

April 22, 2012, 10:00 p.m.—Lauderville

CHARLIE WAS A BELLY-UP-TO-THE-BAR KIND OF GUY, so he was sitting at the counter with his back to the windows. He had ordered a coffee and a tall OJ and was now looking over the menu.

Behind him, a family seemed to be having a difficult time with their young daughter. She looked to be two or three, and she was not letting up with a tantrum. The man got up in a hurry and headed to the restroom, leaving the mother alone. Charlie felt bad for the whole situation. It seemed a bit late to have a small one out.

Finally, he spun around in his bar stool and offered a kind smile. "Hi there, ma'am," he said to the woman. His hand went up to tip his Stetson before he remembered it wasn't there. "Can I be of any assistance? Your little girl seems a might upset."

The child looked at him carefully, then her eyes widened with recognition. "Man with hat! No hat now, but man with hat! He laugh at me! He like me!" she shouted. Her face brightened, yet she was still distraught. She almost seemed to be pleading with him.

Charlie stared back at the little girl in surprise. How did she know he was supposed to have a hat? Something about her seemed familiar, but he couldn't place it. After all, he didn't recognize the mother, and he had never been in this town before.

The girl's mother was getting very agitated. Her eyes darted nervously. She didn't answer Charlie but rather put her hand over the child's mouth in a desperate attempt to quiet her. Charlie couldn't believe it when the child bit the mother's hand.

The mother yelped in pain. She took those two little hands in hers and squeezed them tightly. "No!" she said to the screaming little girl. The more the girl screamed, the harder the mother squeezed.

Charlie now knew he had to intervene. He stood up, his tall frame looming over the booth.

"Ma'am, I believe you are hurting that child. I really think you could be more—"

At that moment, Charlie felt a rough tap on the shoulder. When he turned, a man was right in his face. It was the girl's father.

"Why are you botherin' my family, man? It's none of yer business, now is it? So git on and leave us alone, if you know what's good for you."

The manager looked up from the cash register to see the two men standing face-to-face. "What's going on here?" he said sternly. When neither of them answered, he pulled out his cell phone.

"Man like me! He laugh!" the girl screamed again. "I want my mommy, my daddy, my JJ!"

Hearing the name JJ, everything clicked for Charlie. JJ was Jonas's son. He could suddenly place this little blond girl in Abemly Shores—he remembered seeing her through a window. And yes, he had been wearing his hat that day. Was this Jonas's daughter? Then who were these people?

He looked down at the woman, and her guilty eyes said it all.

"Oh my God," Charlie said out loud.

He reached out for the girl—right as Jack's fist met the side of his jaw. Charlie staggered back and cupped his jaw, moving it around. His eyes were steel.

"Ah sir, I wasn't lookin' for a fight, but apparently it was lookin' for me!" he said, grabbing Jack's collar and returning a jab to his jaw.

Jack lunged at him full bore. His flying fist caught Charlie on the side of the head, near his ear. Charlie groaned and hit the floor hard.

The pain—like nothing he'd felt before. Something warm pooled under him. He couldn't lift himself up. He could only watch as the child screamed and the woman clutched her in fear.

"Jack, no!" the woman shouted. She whirled around in panic, looking out the window. "They're gonna call the cops now! You don't understand—the cops can't find us! They can't see Eden!"

Jack looked at his wife in confusion, then looked down at all the blood under Charlie. The manager came at him, but then froze when Jack brandished a clenched fist.

From the floor, Charlie saw Jack scoop the girl into his arms. As he and the woman ran toward the door, Charlie's eyes closed.

He was out.

Chapter 35

HERO

April 22, 2012, 10:15 p.m.—Lauderville

CHARLIE WOKE TO THE SCREAMS OF SIRENS. When he opened his eyes, bright lights whirled outside the restaurant, coming in through the windows. The sensory overload didn't do his head any good at all. Slowly, he sat up and put a hand to his aching ear. When he pulled the hand back, it was covered in blood.

"What the—?" he mumbled.

Then he remembered the fight. The little girl. He tried to scramble to his feet, but firm hands gently settled him back down. A police officer was hovering over him.

"Sir, sir—it's all right. Please stay down. We have the situation under control. The girl is safe. And an ambulance is on its way for you."

Charlie let out a deep breath. The girl was safe. That was all that mattered.

"Sir, what's your name?" the officer asked.

For a second, Charlie paused. Not long ago, he would have said Chuck Houston. That was the name he had been going by for nine long years, while his memories and life had been hidden from him in a fog. But now the fog had lifted.

"I'm Charlie Tanum," he said with a smile.

"Well, Charlie Tanum," the policeman said, "you are a hero. That little girl had been abducted. And thanks to your bravery to stand up to the couple, we had enough time to get here before they could flee the scene. You will be receiving a medal for the rescue of that little girl. In the meantime, though, your ride is pulling up." He pointed to an ambulance rushing into the parking lot. "Just sit tight till they come and get you. Is there any next of kin we can contact for you?"

"Ah, yes—that would be Cassie Sands Tanum, my wife." It felt good to say that too. He winked at the officer, then let the EMTs lift him onto the stretcher.

As they carried him to the ambulance, Charlie looked over to see the little blond girl smiling at him from the safety of a female police officer's arms. Next he looked over to see the man and woman being read their rights. It appeared, though, that the woman did not want to exercise her right to remain silent.

"Please!" she cried. "Don't take her away! Eden is better off with us! I found her at the park. She was hiding from that teenage boy! She needs a father and a mother who will love her and protect her!"

All the while, her husband just stared into space, his face hollow. Charlie had the sense that he was as shell shocked as everyone else.

An officer responded to the woman by tightening her handcuffs. "Cheylene Grogan, you and your husband, Jack, are under arrest for kidnapping. Get in the car."

Just as the Grogans disappeared into the squad car, Jonas and Savannah turned into the Waffle House parking lot. They had received a call from the police saying that Lily had been found and that she was now safe and out of harm's way. She had been rescued thanks to the heroic efforts of a man named Charlie Tanum.

Savannah craned her neck to search through the lights and police uniforms. "Jonas, do you see her, our baby girl?"

Then she pointed to an ambulance. An EMT was getting ready to close the door.

"Who are they taking in the ambulance? Someone must be hurt!" Becoming frantic again, she whimpered, "Please don't let it be my Lily! She's been through enough. She has to be all right!"

Jonas stopped the car just in time to get a glimpse inside the ambulance. He was surprised to see Slim, the singing cowboy. He didn't look good. Even with his ear bandaged, blood had soaked through. It was matting in his hair and down his neck.

"Oh man! That's Slim—the guy who's been singing at the café! But what is he doing here? I hope he's okay."

Seeing Jonas, Slim smiled at them, trying to raise a hand to wave. Then the door closed, and the ambulance headed to the hospital.

"Jonas!" Savannah suddenly shouted. "There she is! I see our little Lily! Over there in the diner—an officer is holding her!"

Savannah jumped out of the car and took off running toward the little girl wearing a big smile through her tears. Lily jumped down from the officer and opened her arms wide.

"Lily, baby!" Savannah exclaimed. She took Lily in her arms and squeezed her tight.

The officer smiled in joy at seeing the reunion. Savannah mouthed "Thank you" to her, and the officer wiped tears from her eyes. In fact, several of the officers witnessing the scene had to do the same.

"Oh baby, I love you so much!" Savannah said, wrapping Lily in her arms even tighter.

"Mommy, I love you *sooo* much too! I miss you *sooo* much!" She let out a little giggle. "Mommy tickling Lily, holding Lily so tight!"

There was another giggle as she saw Jonas coming toward her. She opened her arms again. "Daddy, Daddy! Man with hat like me! He help Lily," she said with a big smile.

Savannah gave Jonas a confused look. "What man with a hat?" she said.

Jonas could only return the confused look for a moment. "I don't know—but wait. I think I remember her talking about this man with a hat yesterday too."

Savannah laughed and shook her head. "I'm so confused! I guess that means I've been away much too long. But all that matters is that we have our Lily back!" She gave the child a kiss through happy tears.

Jonas joined in with the kisses and hugs, then turned to the officers. "Someone told us a Charlie Tanum helped save Lily. Is he here? We'd love to meet him and thank him."

"Actually, the ambulance just took him to the hospital," said one of the officers. "He was in an altercation with the kidnappers, and he sustained an injury."

It took several seconds for that to sink in for Jonas. He stood frozen for a moment, then he turned his head in the direction he'd seen the ambulance leave.

"Slim?" he finally said. "Slim is Charlie Tanum? But I thought he said his name was Chuck Houston." He paused again. "Are you saying Slim rescued Lily?"

"Man with hat!" Lily said again, as if confirming her father's question.

Jonas suddenly remembered Slim's signature Stetson. Maybe he *was* the man with the hat. But had Slim even met Lily? How did she know him? And how in the world did he manage to be at this Waffle House right in time to save Lily? There were so many unanswered questions.

Jonas just shrugged and laughed. "Well, I hope we'll someday get to the bottom of this mystery about Charlie, or Chuck, or Slim, or the man with the hat!"

Little did Jonas know just what else that mystery would reveal.

Chapter 36

TWIST OF FATE

April 30, 2012—Abemly Shores

IN THE LOCAL HOSPITAL, CASSIE SAT at Charlie's bedside. She held his hand and watched him sleep. She reached out to brush back that wisp of hair that always fell across his eyes.

The surgery had successfully removed a benign mass that had been pressing on a nerve in his brain and impairing his memory for years. The mass had been slow growing, but it had apparently started while he was on assignment in DC. It had been enough to cause amnesia and keep him from finding his way back to Cassie or anyone he knew.

But by some remarkable twist of fate, he had been guided to the sleepy little town of Abemly Shores to save a little girl's life and rekindle his own.

Or maybe it had been just something in the wind.

Epilogue

July 4, 2013—Abemly Shores

FOURTH OF JULY AT THE BECKMAN COTTAGE had become a tradition, just as it had been with the Sillses. It was a day of celebration and good food made by the grill master and, of course, his assistant.

The flower garden at the bottom of the porch steps was in full bloom, and flowers continued to trickle down the walking path. Baby pools were scattered around for the young children—or any guests who wanted to dip their toes and cool off in a hurry.

The bridge women mingled on the large porch while the teens played Frisbee and beach volleyball closer to the ocean. As always, there was a serious game of horseshoes. The croquet sets were out on the lawn as well. And we can't forget about the three-legged races and beanbag toss.

The day was a brilliant ninety degrees—sunny with an enchanting breeze mingling amongst the guests. Performing her graceful assemblés and sweeping balancés, the breeze comforted her guests as the light scent of honeysuckle tiptoed in the air.

Jonathon Sills and Hal Sheridan were setting up the camera on the porch to take family pictures of the guests. The birthday girl, Lily, was pleased as punch to be their model and assistant.

"Hal," Jonathon said, "don't you think Lily is the most beautiful four-year-old birthday girl model you've ever seen?"

"Absolutely! And I'm not one bit prejudiced because she's my granddaughter." He bent down to give Lily a hug. Their mirrored hazel eyes beamed. "Hey, big girl—remind me again how old you are today."

"Grandpa Hal, you already know! I'm four, and it's the Fourth of July! JJ said this is my golden birthday. That means I can wish for something really special. He said that's what he got to do for his golden birthday. And his wish even came true!" Pointing to herself, she announced, "He wished for *me*! He says he loves me bunches. I was his best present ever!"

Just then, JJ and Joey Sands walked over. JJ swept Lily up and swung her around. She shrieked with giggles.

"Lily, you are the giggliest girl I know! I love you! Happy fourth birthday!"

Lily planted a big kiss on her brother, then turned to Joey. "When is Cassie coming? I have a secret to ask her." She put her finger to her lips in a shush gesture.

"She and Uncle Charlie said they'd be here by noon. You won't have too long to wait, kid," Joey said, giving her blond curls a gentle toss.

Lily glanced over to spot Dotty Sheridan hugging Cecilia Sills and Mona Argyle. Lily skipped off to greet them. She ran into Dotty's arms.

"Grandma Dot, Grandma Dot! Today is my golden birthday. I'm going to ask for something very special!"

Dotty knelt down to give her a hug. "And what might that be, my sweet girl?"

"*Sh!*" Lily giggled. "It's a secret! I can't share, or it won't come true."

Twirling a blond curl around her finger, Dotty whispered, "I understand completely. I wouldn't think of spoiling your secret. I promise not to say another word about it." She stood and winked at the other women.

"Oh look—Cassie and Charlie just arrived," Mona said, waving at them. "Will you excuse me, please? I have to speak to Charlie about something."

"'Scuse me too, please," Lily spoke up, trying her best to sound like a big girl. "I have to speak to Cassie. Can I come with you, Mona?"

"Of course you can, little one." She took Lily's hand in hers.

After a few steps, Lily tugged at Mona's arm. "Do you know Cassie has a baby in her tummy?" she whispered.

"Yes, I do. Isn't it wonderful?"

As they got closer, Lily ran over to Cassie, who simply glowed. Mona went to give Charlie a hug.

"May I have a few minutes of your time, good sir?" she asked with a smile.

Charlie put his arm around Mona, then turned to wink at Cassie before Mona ushered him away.

"Why yes, milady?" he said with an outpouring of his charismatic charm. He tipped his Stetson, which was now properly right where it belonged—on his head. "You know, I'd do anything for ya, darlin'."

"Charlie, I never got the chance to properly thank you for the article you wrote honoring my Easton." She paused to dab at her eyes with a tissue. "All those years ago, when they came to tell me he had been killed in Vietnam, I thought I'd stop breathing. But with the love and support of friends and family, I was able to go on with my life."

Mona took something from her pocket.

"This is the medal he earned his senior year of high school. It was for an article he wrote honoring war correspondents." She placed the medal in the palm of Charlie's hand. "I was deeply touched by the amount of research you did to present such a heartfelt tribute to a very special person in my life. The things you wrote brought back all the beauty of Easton for me. So please accept this medal from him to you. You see, he was planning on going to college to become a journalist after he came back from the war."

Charlie closed his fingers over the medal. For a moment, the lump in his throat caused him to choke on his words. He kissed the top of Mona's head and smiled.

"It was a privilege to write about your brave soldier, Mona. It would also be a privilege if you would someday allow me to read the article he wrote—when you are ready, of course." He tipped his hat again and walked back toward his wife, clutching the medal in his hand.

Charlie broke into a grin when he saw Lily standing with her tiny hand on Cassie's belly, apparently whispering to the life inside. She let out yet another giggle, then hugged Cassie before scurrying off to find her parents.

"Is it time to ask for my golden birthday wish?" she asked breathlessly when she found Savannah and Jonas on the porch.

"Absolutely," Jonas replied. "You can ask away, birthday girl!"

Lily drew in a huge breath. "Mommy, Daddy . . . what I really want for my golden birthday is a baby sister or brother. It's just like what JJ asked for on his special birthday—and he got me!"

Savannah felt a sudden warmth near her heart. She placed her hand over the necklace Jonas had made for her out of that very special white stone. Without a word, she took Jonas's hand in hers. They smiled at each other as their eyes twinkled.

Just then, a damp, gentle mist filled the air. It was followed by a radiant rainbow. A sweeping breeze performed a series of pirouettes and finally a curtsy before leaving the faint aroma of honeysuckle in her wake.

Acknowledgments

THANK YOU TO MY FAMILY AND FRIENDS who have supported and encouraged me on this amazing journey. I'm grateful to all of you for helping me bring Abemly Shores to life.

To my editor, Angie Wiechmann—I can't thank you enough for your expertise and guidance in taking me through this process from beginning to "The End."

Thank you to Hanna, Athena, and Beaver's Pond Press.

May the winds of Abemly always be with you.